"So," she said, "it will be good to start at the market before sunrise. You will buy all the clothes I need, then bring them here. I will dress and we will leave. But you must hurry. Sunrise will be in about half an hour."

"The maid will come in very early with my washed clothes," Slocum said.

"I will be in your bed. She will think I am a whore you took back with you."

Slocum laughed, admiring her bluntness.

"Now, go to the market," she ordered.

"There is no way I can buy clothes for you till I see your body."

She had not considered this. She flushed. "Yes," she said finally, "that is true."

It was no time for false modesty. She stripped off her dress. Underneath she wore only a coarse white cotton undergarment with a severe high neck. It fitted her tightly. She had a ripe body for an Apache woman . . .

JAKE LOGAN

BANDIT GOLD

BERKLEY BOOKS, NEW YORK

BANDIT GOLD

A Berkley Book / published by arrangement with
the author

PRINTING HISTORY
Berkley edition / May 1984

ISBN: 0-425-07018-2

A BERKLEY BOOK ® TM 757,375
Berkley Books are published by The Berkley Publishing Group,
200 Madison Avenue, New York, N.Y. 10016.
The name "BERKLEY" and the stylized "B" with design are trademarks
belonging to Berkley Publishing Corporation.
PRINTED IN THE UNITED STATES OF AMERICA

BANDIT GOLD

1

John Slocum bent over Father Gregorio. The old priest, who had been born in Andalucía ninety years before, was breathing in a harsh, ragged manner. He was lying on his back with his eyes closed, on the stone floor of the chapel of the abandoned mission of Nuestra Señora de Los Rios—Our Lady of the Rivers. The priest wore only a thin brown robe to cover his emaciated, shivering body. He was barefoot. He made a practice of sleeping this way in order to do penance for his sins.

Slocum had come across the tiny old mission on his way to Mexico. He had not even known it was there. From the crest of the range that fringed the river valley to the east he had seen the green meadows, lush with grass, surrounding the collapsed bell tower. He decided that his horse could use some of that good grass and he himself might be able

1

to pick off a few quail with the shotgun he carried disassembled in his saddlebag. Fresh broiled quail would taste damn good after the jerky he had been eating during the three weeks he had been riding south from western Nebraska.

His other diet had been the road agent special, rice and raisins cooked together. It was quickly prepared and nourishing, and could be eaten cold by a man making time on horseback. But fresh meat was what he wanted right now.

So he had ridden down, splashed across the shallow, reed-bordered river, and stripped the saddle and blanket off Old Joe, his five-year-old sorrel. Old Joe rolled on his back in ecstasy before he began to munch the grass.

Sure enough, there was quail—the brown and white Gambel's quail that had just flown in from the nearby desert to water. Slocum put his shotgun together and slipped in two shells. He began walking across the meadow and immediately flushed five quail. Two quick snap shots and two of them went down. In fifteen minutes he had stripped their feathers, gutted them, rubbed a pinch of salt over them, spitted them on a two foot length of stiff wire he carried for the purpose, and was broiling them over a fire made from some wood he had found at the river's edge.

The quail were plump and juicy. After Slocum had gnawed the last bone he took his sweat-soaked saddle blanket and washed it in the river with the bar of brown laundry soap he always carried in his saddlebag. He laid the blanket out on the grass. The hot sun would dry it quickly, and while it was drying he decided to explore what he thought was an abandoned mission. He explored the outbuildings first and then approached the chapel. As soon as he opened the rotting wooden door he heard Father Gregorio moaning for water in the stifling interior.

Slocum gave the old priest some water from his canteen. Next he placed the emaciated old man on his sun-dried saddle blanket under an *alamo*—an old cottonwood tree growing next to the chapel wall. There a cool breeze blew constantly from the river.

The old man had recovered a little. When Slocum warmed up his road agent special and fed Father Gregorio with the battered spoon he carried in his saddlebag, the priest smiled and said weakly, *"Muchas gracias, hijo mio."*

"Por nada," Slocum replied.

"Mejicano?" the priest asked.

"No, padre. Soy gringo."

The old man laughed. "God will reward you, nevertheless."

Slocum doubted that. He had not put his faith in God in all his years of roaming from Montana to Mexico, from California east to Nebraska. He relied upon himself without heavenly help. That was how he had survived as a rebel officer and later, as he roamed everywhere in the West. But he had no wish to offend the old man, so all he said was, "Thank you, Father."

Father Gregorio's gaze had fixed itself upon Slocum's tanned face and hard jaw. Slocum hadn't bothered to shave since he had left Nebraska in a hurry when one of his men got drunk in a saloon and boasted how he and Slocum had lifted a hundred and twenty prime cattle from the Palmer Ranch. Sam Palmer carried a lot of weight in Nebraska, and Slocum had lit out so quickly that he had had no time to visit his safe deposit box in the Cattlemen's Bank in Niobrara. By now it would have been sequestered by the marshal anyway. Write it off as experience, Slocum told himself.

"You are a good man," Father Gregorio said to him.

Slocum shrugged. He had his doubts. After he had left Niobrara he rode south to the Platte. Then he went across Cheyenne country to the Cimarron. He took a chance and used the Cimarron cutoff of the Santa Fe trail as far as Fort Union in New Mexico, then he headed southwest to San Ildefonso Pueblo. Pueblo Indians had no interest in white men's law as long as a man behaved in their country. He moved down the pueblo chain to Cochiti, then Laguna and Acoma, politely received in each place.

Then he rode past Magdalena and Datil, across the high pine forest of the Continental Divide, crossed the trail blazed by Coronado in 1540, and then angled southwest to avoid the Chiricahua Apache country.

And thus he came to the mission of Our Lady of the Rivers, so called because it had been built at the meeting place of two rivers.

"I am a very old man at the end of my life," Father Gregorio said. He stared up at Slocum's sunburned, unshaven face. "I ask you, a stranger and an American, to do me a great favor." He reached out and took Slocum's big right hand in his two small, frail ones, freckled with age spots. He held on tightly, the way a young child would. Slocum was touched.

"Will you do me this favor?" the priest asked.

Slocum was always wary of jumping into a situation without careful thought. He was about to say no when Father Gregorio said calmly, "I will die soon. I am alone here. There is no one left to ask. You are a hard man but a man of honor. We Spaniards say *palabra de Ingles,* word of an Englishman, when we mean word of honor. You are English in ancestry, so I know you will not give a promise just to make a dying man keep quiet. If you make a promise, you will keep it. This I know."

Slocum cursed silently. The old man was right.

"So, *hijo mio,* promise me, or go. Which is it?"

Slocum was silent.

"Suppose I tell you what it is about first. That is fair, no?"

Slocum said with relief, "Yes."

The telling would give him a way out, he was sure.

2

"Está bien," the old priest began. "Sixty-five years ago this was a beautiful place. Many happy Indians had become Christians. We grew everything we needed; watermelons, onions, tomatoes, and corn. Fat cattle grazed in the meadows out there, fine bells cast in Spain hung in the belfry, brought up from Chihuahua by ox cart. In the mountains were rich gold mines. The mine owners were grateful to God for their good fortune, so the carvings inside this chapel were covered with gold leaf. The altar was oak and carved with scenes of the procession up the Via Dolorosa. The ceiling here was covered with gold.

"They cast many great golden candlesticks of pure gold for our chapel. And they carved the statue of the Virgin there—do you see her?"

Slocum turned. In the dim light he became aware of a life-sized carved wooden statue of the Virgin at the far end of the chapel.

"Yes," he said.

"Now she looks like a poor girl, but in the old days she wore a robe of such richness you would not believe it. Not even Queen Isabella had one like it! It was woven with gold and silver thread by my Pimas. All over it were sewn diamonds, and emeralds from Colombia carried here overland from Darien. There were rubies from Burma brought to Mexico by the Manila galleons. And pearls—such pearls they were!—from the Sea of Cortez. You call it the Gulf of California. Big rose pearls, some of them as big as cherries.

"When the robe was put on, Indians came from far to pray to her for miracles. And Our Lady of the Rivers granted them, so pleased was she with her robe and her candlesticks.

"And so I was very happy. But then the raids began."

"The raids?" Slocum asked.

"The Apaches. Some say the Comanches were pressing them from the east and the Utes were pushing them from the north, so they came to this country. They killed many ranchers and many miners, and the soldiers sent up from Mexico were so few that one day my bishop ordered all the missions to fall back to Chihauhua. This meant I had to abandon Our Lady of the Rivers.

"So the Papagoes and then the Pimas left. And then I and an old Huastecan Indian were the only ones left here. I say Juanito was old, but that was because I myself was only thirty then. In reality he was fifty or so, I suppose. I thought *that* was old!"

Father Gregorio's laugh turned into convulsive coughing. When he recovered he went on.

"You understand, now that I am nearly ninety years old, how foolish I was. Apaches were everywhere, killing the cattle, eating our watermelons and tomatoes right from the little garden here. They still bore some awe towards me; they knew I was a holy man, but I never knew when one of them might suddenly decide to kill me. Because, you see, many Spaniards had done terrible things to them. Water, please."

Slocum held the man's fragile shoulders while Father Gregorio sipped. Then the priest continued, with many pauses while he struggled for breath. He was visibly growing weaker. His story, as Slocum pieced it together over the next hour, held Slocum riveted.

Father Gregorio knew that an Apache raid could be mounted at any time. But Apaches did not like to move at night. The priest explained that was becuase they believed that the ghosts of their ancestors were everywhere; they were frequently malevolent, and might choose to release evil. So Apaches preferred to raid at dawn.

Father Gregorio, therefore, waited for a night of hard rain when the visibility would be low. It was late winter, and there were frequent heavy rains. He had prepared by wrapping the great gold candlesticks in heavy burlap bags. He had carefully removed the jeweled robe from the Virgin and wrapped it in cotton cloth of the type given to the women so they could clothe their shameful nakedness. He put the robe into another burlap bag. Then he performed one more operation upon the Virgin while the Huastecan Indian was asleep. Father Gregorio believed firmly that a secret shared becomes public property.

A fence-lifter came along two nights later. At its height they mounted their mules, loaded the two pack mules, and swum them across the river, and then up into the mountains east of the mission. Father Gregorio preferred the sure-footed mules for mountain travel to any horse, no matter how noble its lineage. Once in the mountains, Father Gregorio went directly to a small mine opening he knew. Long before a miner had sunk an exploratory shaft there, but he had soon abandoned it in disgust.

It was dry inside. The two men dragged the heavy burlap sacks from the mules and set them down inside the opening. Then they filled the opening with rocks, plastered mud between and around them, and next transplanted small piñon trees and set them in the mud. They would take very nicely in their new setting. Grass seeds would blow onto the mud, and soon the opening would look just like any other hillside in southern Arizona.

The rain lasted all through their work. Half an hour later the sun was rising. The mission was surrounded with Chiricahua Apaches, all painted black for war. As Father Gregorio and Juanito watched, the Apaches burst into the mission. They were furious because their prey had fled. The rain had washed out any tracks the two might have left. The Apaches burned the altar and set fire to the building, but the statue of the Virgin refused to burn. It was a miracle, Father Gregorio said.

"*Claro,*" Slocum said gravely.

Father Gregorio smiled. "*Claro,*" he whispered.

After hiding all day he and the Huastecan set out on the three-hundred-mile trip to Chihuahua. Two days later, while Juanito was hunting rabbits with a club—for they carried no weapons—two Apaches seized him. They took him with them, tortured him intermittently for a few hours, and then killed him.

Father Gregorio waited for Juanito for two days, and

then went on alone. Almost immediately he found Juanito's body. He spent several hours digging a grave with a pointed, fire-hardened stick, even though it was dangerous to spend so much time in daylight in Apache territory.

With Juanito buried and the grave covered with heavy stones to discourage scavenging coyotes, Father Gregorio rode on to Chihuahua. He moved only at night. When he reported to Bishop Tomás Herrera he was burned to a deep copper color and he weighed only 114 pounds.

The bishop considered the abandoned mission an embarrassment. The Holy Father took a dim view of such constant losses, and Herrera knew there would be papal emissaries going back and forth from Rome to Mexico City demanding explanations. With complete injustice, Bishop Herrera accused Father Gregorio of slipshod administration and deliberate alienation of the Apaches.

When the stunned priest said he did not understand, the bishop asked why he had pampered the Pimas and Papagoes rather than the Apaches.

Father Gregorio said he did not understand the question.

"I shall be very clear," Bishop Herrera said coldly. "The Apaches have effectively removed Arizona from the grasp of Mother Church. Their enemies are the Pimas and Papagoes. These are sedentary Indians. They are not numerous at all. Why, therefore, have you not made friends of the Apaches?"

"I tried to make Christians of them all," Father Greg said in all sincerity.

"A mistake," Herrera said. "It was a mistake to send an incompetent romantic such as you to that important area. You are hereby assigned to San Andres Chalchicomula. You will leave tomorrow."

"But that is in Guatemala!" Father Gregorio protested.

"Exactly. I do not wish to see nor hear from you," the bishop replied.

He held out his hand. Father Gregorio, puzzled, humiliated, and angry, kissed the bishop's ring and left. He had intended to tell the bishop where he had hidden the treasure of the Virgin. But now that he had been dismissed in such an insulting manner, and so injustly, Father Gregorio decided to keep the secret to himself until another bishop would be sent to Chihuahua. There was only one other person who had known—and he was buried in a simple grave far to the north.

So Father Gregorio went off to the hot, humid Guatemalan rain forest, where he ministered to the spiritual wants of a few Mayas. For forty years he labored every day. Herrera lived on, still bishop. Then one day Father Gregorio wrote for permission to visit his home in Andalucía. It was the only time in his life he had ever asked for a vacation, and he was granted six months' leave.

Following orders, he traveled to Vera Cruz. There he stayed in a monastery while he waited for a ship that would be sailing to Cadiz. He had been given enough money for the round trip, and enough to live on decently when in Spain.

But his ship the San Ignacio, would be delayed for one month in Havana for repairs.

Things were relatively peaceful now in Arizona. The Americans now owned Arizona and constantly patrolled the roads. Transportation had improved enormously as well. Father Gregorio suddenly decided to see Nuestra Señora de los Rios, his old mission, once more. Without notifying anyone he bought laymen's clothes, put them on, and took the train and stagecoach to the north. In seven days he was once more in Arizona.

His heart beat wildly when he saw Nuestra Señora de

los Rios once more. The place was still in ruins, but the meadows were rich with grass and the rivers still flowed. He had planned to stay there for the afternoon and then ride his rented horse back to Tucson, from where he would go south once more to Vera Cruz and board the ship.

But he stayed. He stayed there past his six-month vacation.

By then he had cleaned out the debris of forty years of neglect, wild animals, and arson. From the belfry he took the bat guano, which he used for the garden he started once more next to the chapel wall.

Some old Indians, who remembered the priest with affection, gave him a goat so that he could make cheese. He could not go back to Guatemala and abandon the goat. Besides, if he were to go back, who would repair the mission? If the Church had abandoned her, he had not.

No one in the hierarchy knew where he was. They had found out soon enough that he had not sailed on the *San Ignacio*. They deduced that some waterfront scoundrel had found out that Father Gregorio had plenty of money, killed him with a knife in the ribs, and then dumped his body into the harbor, where the sharks must have disposed of the body quickly.

No one would ever think that he had returned to Nuestra Señora de los Rios.

One day, years later, a traveler stopped for tomatoes and left some newspapers from Mexico City. In one of them a Bishop Serdan was mentioned. So there was a new bishop! But Father Gregorio did not really care any more. It was all so far away. What he wanted to do was to restore the chapel, little by little, to its former glory, gold leaf and all.

And when that was done he would open the hidden mine and put the candlesticks and the jeweled robe where they belonged. That would make the Holy Father sit up and take notice!

But then he realized he had disobeyed the orders of his superiors. For that he devised a penance for himself: he would sleep on the bare stone floor of the chapel and walk barefoot, even among the cactus and no matter how hot the soil was. This he would do until the day the Holy Father would forgive him.

One morning he was making adobe bricks at a clay deposit beside the river. He suddenly heard a faint wail across the river. He hoisted up his brown robe and waded across. There he found a six-month-old baby Apache girl in a cradle board. She was covered with the dull red spots of measles. Beside her there were moccasin tracks. The moccasin pattern was clearly Chiricahua Apache.

Measles was a white man's children's disease. Trivial enough to white children, it was deadly to Indian children who had not built up a racial immunity. There was no way to treat it. If anyone died in an Apache camp the *jacal* where the death occurred was immediately burned and the whole camp moved in order to avoid the vengeful ghost. And even babies had ghosts. In the long run, Father Gregorio supposed, abandoning the baby girl was the most sensible solution if the band's total welfare were considered. Nevertheless, Father Gregorio, during his tenure, had always fought this custom as hard as he could, and God only knew how many babies had been exposed on remote mountain hillsides.

Still, finding one alive was a sort of miracle. Usually they died alone in some isolated area, far from any trail. Father Gregorio, in his rare travels to one of the villages, had occasionally run across what was left after the coyotes and *zapilotes* had been at work.

So the baby became a challenge to him. He pulled her from the cradle board. She was naked and screaming lustily. A good sign—she was not very sick. Father Gregorio smiled. She was a strong little thing, a wild Apache, not like the tame Papagoes. He bathed her gently in the river until he washed her clean. And he suddenly decided to baptize her. She would be his sole Apache convert, but he did not know that yet.

He made the sign of the cross, and then said, "I baptize thee Pilar de los Rios, in the name of the Father, and of the Son, and of the Holy Ghost." Pilar for his mother, and de los Rios for the mission.

He spread a blanket under a cottonwood tree. By chance, it was the same cottonwood where Slocum would set down the ancient priest many years later. As the cool wind blew across the baby, he dipped a clean cotton rag into a clay pot with incised designs which had somehow come all the way down from Santa Clara, traded from tribe to tribe. She sucked greedily at the goat's milk. Then she fell asleep. She was a beautiful little thing, thought Father Gregorio, with eyes the color of wet black stones, straight legs, and sturdy shoulders.

Much to his delight she survived.

When she was well, the priest approached the Pima and Papago women who occasionally passed by the mission. No one would adopt her. She was a hated Chiricahua Apache. The band which had abandoned her had gone on deep into the Sierra Madres of northern Mexico. They never passed by the mission again.

So he assumed responsibility for her. While he slowly rebuilt the chapel, replacing the roofbeams with wood he cut in the mountains and dragged to the mission with his two oxen given to him by the Papagoes, she walked beside him. From the time she was two years old she could walk without tiring.

Father Gregorio had come from an old family with aristocratic lineage. He spoke the classical, majestic Spanish of old Castile. This he taught to her as they walked. She grew up speaking flawless Castilian. She knew no other language.

Clothes were a problem. Once a year a reliable trader stopped on his way north. Father Gregorio left a standing order with him for simple dresses that would fit Pilar. He paid for them with goat cheese and fresh vegetables from the garden. By the time she was seven Pilar spoke perfect Spanish and could read and write with ease. The old priest could see she would become a stunning beauty when she would reach her full growth.

He knew something had to be done about her future. She loved him like a real father, but he would have to send her away. She would have to grow up with other children; it was not good for her to know only the companionship of an old man and a few goats.

In Hermosillo was the Convent of the Sacred Heart. He had heard that the Mother Superior there was both kind and intelligent. The next visit by the Mexican trader would be in a week. Father Gregorio sat down and wrote a letter to the Mother Superior. He wrote about finding Pilar, and he asked that she be brought up a devout Catholic woman. Then he told Pilar she would be living in a convent and how much she would like playing with other girls. She burst into tears. It was hard to resist her frantic appeals to stay with him, but resist he did.

When the trader, Don Manuel Valverde, came by, Father Gregorio said to him, "You will take Pilar with you to the

Convent of the Sacred Heart. I commend her to your care. Do you accept?"

If he accepted, this would mean a long extra trip across the Sierra Madres from Chihuahua. By saying he commended Pilar to Valverde's care Father Gregorio had asked and expected Valverde to protect her with his life, if need be.

Valverde hesitated. The extra trip would take three weeks out of his life. He had no business to conduct in Hermosillo. Father Gregorio then leaned over and placed a small leather pouch in Valverde's hand. It contained the gold coins which had been intended for the old man's vacation in Spain.

"This is not necessary," Valverde said stiffly.

"Take it. You will have expenses," the priest insisted.

This was true. Valverde was always accompanied by an armed escort. He turned and looked at Pilar, who liked him. She had not even looked at the new dresses he bought for her. From the beginning he had always brought a doll or a toy on each trip. He felt sorry for the abandoned, motherless Apache girl.

"All right," Valverde finally said.

In the morning, Father Gregorio bent down and lifted Pilar onto the horse Valverde provided. She had been crying all night and would not look at him.

"You will come back one day," he told the sobbing girl. "And then you will see how beautiful our mission will be! And the treasure of the Virgin—it is hidden. She will take it out for us. But who knows where it is now?"

She stopped crying and stared at him.

He tapped his head and pointed to the statue of the Virgin inside the chapel, smiling down in the darkness. "Believe, Pilar. She knows where it is. And now, go with God. Do not turn around."

So Pilar rode away to Hermosillo.

3

"That," Father Gregorio told Slocum, "was almost twenty years ago. She wrote two or three times, then the letters stopped. I think the reason was that the Mother Superior discovered that I had violated my vows of obedience. Please see if Pilar is still there. If she is, tell her to come here once more. And then she shall have the treasure of the Virgin for her convent. I am too old and too foolish to do anything with it here. I cannot finish my work. I know what you think. The foolish old man will be dead by the time she comes here. But I am far stronger than I look. I will improve. I know."

Slocum had his doubts.

"In the chapel, beside the altar, is a box. Inside is pen, ink, paper. Bring it here, please."

Slocum picked up the box. The Virgin smiled secretly

at him from above. She knew plenty, Slocum thought, but she wasn't talking. Not to him.

When he brought out the box Father Gregorio sat up with Slocum's help. He leaned against the tree trunk and wrote a brief note. Slocum folded it carefully. Later he would wrap it in a square of oiled silk he kept in the bottom of one of his two saddlebags.

"Well, then, *amigo! Adios y muchas gracias.*"

And so Slocum set out on a ride of two hundred and fifty miles to Hermosillo. He liked the old priest, but he liked even more the comforting thought that the treasure of the Virgin, if properly handled, might well become the treasure of John Slocum. He grinned. If he laid hands on it, it would make his hasty ride from Nebraska and the accidental meeting with the old priest a very profitable venture. A lot depended on Pilar de los Rios, though.

Slocum dropped down across the border into Mexico. Two days' easy riding brought him to Tubutama. The next night he slept in Magdalena, far enough to the west of the Rio Sonora so that he did not have to keep a constant lookout for any Apache war party that might be breaking out of the Sierra Madre. Four more days of hard riding brought him to Hermosillo hot, filthy and badly in need of a bath and a shave and clean clothes. He found a livery stable, took a cheap room nearby, and had a bath and a shave. That done, he pulled a clean shirt and a clean pair of pants from his saddlebag and asked the way to the Convent of the Sacred Heart. Told with some surprise that it was close—what did a man like him want with a convent?—he walked.

Surrounded by high stone walls with glass shards set into their tops, the building from the outside looked grim and forbidding. Iron-barred windows with wooden shutters behind them broke up the long façade. Slocum lifted the big iron knocker designed like a lion's head and let it drop.

After a minute a small wooden door set low beside the big gate opened. A nun with the wide-winged white coif of the order stood there with her hands clasped in front of her.

Slocum took off his dusty sombrero and bowed. When he wanted to he possessed all the good manners of the upper-class Spaniard. He judged, with her face hidden in the shadow of the coif, that she could be anywhere from thirty to fifty years old.

"Good afternoon, Sister," he said in Spanish.

She lifted a hand in gentle reproff. "Enter, señor," she said softly, in a low contralto Slocum liked. "I am the Mother Superior. It is hot and you are probably thirsty. A cold drink?"

Slocum smiled. She saw a hard brown face with green eyes set deep above the strong nose. A narrow face that had seen plenty. She stepped aside to let him precede her. Inside the patio a fountain was spraying cold water into the air. Flowers grew everywhere. Against one wall a lime tree grew, laden with its tiny green globes. In its shade was an oak bench.

"Please sit," she said. With a lithe movement she reached up and pulled three limes from the branches. Even though she was draped within the folds of her habit, still with her face hidden in shadow, it was easy to see that she had the body of a vigorous, mature woman. Slocum revised his estimate of her age.

He stared at her. He had not slept with a woman for more than two months. And now, he thought ruefully, it was his luck to meet one who could never be available. With a rustle of fabric she turned from the tree and disappeared into the convent with a swift stride. She was quite tall. Slocum liked tall women. He sighed.

With the humming of the bees extracting nectar, the soft splash of the water, and the cool breeze blowing, Slocum fell asleep on the bench.

A hand touched his shoulder gently. Instinct took over and he went into a swift half-crouch. He had his Colt almost out of its holster before he could check himself.

She was standing in front of him with a tall green hand-blown glass in her hand. Pieces of lime pulp were floating on top of the cold liquid. She wore an amused smile.

"I do not think you live a quiet life, señor."

Slocum took the lime drink and begged her pardon. He was embarrassed. The drink was deliciously cold and the bits of pulp burst on his tongue with their tart, sharp flavor.

"No matter," she said. "There are many cruel people in this world. If you have not been strong enough to take the vow of peace, I cannot hold it against you to see you so ready to defend yourself, señor."

He marvelled at her flawless Spanish. Perhaps she was a noblewoman. He still had not seen her face. She smiled, hands clasped in front of her, her eyes downcast while he finished the drink.

Then she held out her hand. The fingers were long, and pale brown; Slocum thought she must spend much time gardening. He gave her the empty glass and their fingers touched. He forced himself not to think of her as a woman.

"And now, señor," she said courteously, "how can I help you?"

He handed her Father Gregorio's note.

She read it carefully. Slocum could not see her face clearly. Then her head lifted and she stared into his eyes.

"Come inside. I will tell you what happened to Pilar de los Rios," she said calmly.

A sudden surge of anger swept through Slocum. No Pilar, no treasure, that long ride for nothing!

"If she's dead, tell me now," he said harshly.

"Come inside" she said gently.

An Indian woman glided up and bowed. She was the fat cook. She started a long-winded complaint about a novice who would not peel potatoes properly.

"Later, Teresa," the nun said firmly. Teresa curtsied and left. The nun was not over thirty at the most, Slocum thought, as he followed her into her office. There was a big mahogany desk with paper in neat stacks. An inkwell, a pen, sand for blotting. Bookcases lined the wall. They were filled with quartos and folios bound in brown calf. Light fell through the high barred windows onto the red tile floors. The place was very quiet. Two black kittens played with an orange-sized ball of fabric scraps.

She sat down in a high-backed chair and placed her brown hand flat on the table.

"Señor," she said "I was Pilar de los Rios. I am now Sister Prudencia. There is nothing I can do about Father Gregorio's wishes. He has lived over fifty years in direct disobedience of his superiors and his order. Do you understand?"

Slocum stood. There was no reason for him to spend a minute more in Hermosillo. Suddenly, as he turned to go, he saw tears sliding down her cheeks.

"Adios, señor," she said.

"Adios, Pilar de los Rios," he said, and walked out.

She sat with her hands clasped at her desk till the sound of his bootheels on the tile floor had died away. No one had called her Pilar for over twenty years. The name flooded her with memories; Father Gregorio holding her tiny hand in his big work-hardened one as he traced out the letters of the alphabet with her. She still remembered his triumphant laugh when she wrote her name for the first time.

"Pilar de los Rios," she had said in awe. "That's me!"

"A beautiful name," he had responded.

Yes, it was a beautiful name. Better than Prudencia. She had never liked that name. It had been chosen for her by the nuns when she had been deposited at the convent by Valverde, who had ridden away and had never come back. She had stared at his retreating horse and cried bitterly. She wrote letters to Father Gregorio, but most were confiscated and burned. There was nowhere else for her to go. No one would consider taking an Indian girl, especially an Apache, except the Church, where an Apache woman who spoke and wrote perfect English and Castilian Spanish could go far. And when it was discovered that she was extremely intelligent and had administrative abilities, her future in high office was assured. So she had pushed the old man out of her mind.

Until the tall American had come. Once more she cried for Father Gregorio. He was an old man, now dying. Would it not be a great sin to deny him?

She stood and clapped her hands. An Indian gardener just outside her office heard and came in, pulling off his straw sombrero. He was intelligent and could be trusted to keep quiet.

She gave him crisp instructions.

4

Slocum had only a few silver pesos left in his pocket. He strolled slowly along the narrow streets till he came to a large open-air market. There he bought two big, ripe tomatoes. He ate them as he walked to the livery stable. Old Joe whinnied when he saw Slocum. The horse had been curried and the oats in his nose bag were decent quality. Satisfied, Slocum next asked for a good hotel. He wanted a long, restful night's sleep on a real mattress before he left in the morning to ride north.

He found a *posada* with a big corner room. The corner held a huge copper tub which the giggling maidservant filled with buckets of hot water.

"Do you desire company, señor?" she asked.

"I am very tired. Perhaps in the morning."

"Understood, señor."

She took away his dirty clothes for washing and ironing.

25

They would be ready early in the morning. He put on his remaining clean shirt and pants and went out to eat. When he came back he pulled off his boots and lay down. He was asleep within five minutes.

"Señor?"

A hand touched him lightly on the shoulder. He came awake swiftly. The voice had been a woman's. It was dark outside. The town's lights had been extinguished. It was very late.

He thought it was the maidservant. "Take off your dress, *querida,*" he said sleepily, patting the bed beside him.

A voice said dryly, "I think not, señor."

He sat bolt upright. It was Pilar de los Rios.

He stared at her in the light that filtered in from a street lamp. The coif and habit were gone. She wore a plain black dress with a black rebozo. Her beauty stunned him.

"Señor, I will go with you to see Father Gregorio," she said.

Slocum had had second thoughts about this. He had entertained the possibility on the way down from Arizona. To travel with a nun would be immensely difficult, not to mention embarrassing. They would attract enormous attention, much of it obscene. Everyone they encountered would be watching every move they made. If they found the treasure, half the Territory would try to take it from them while the other half watched. Besides, they would have to sleep and eat at inns—rare enough on the way north—and Slocum did not have enough money even for himself. This last night at the *posada* would clean him out.

He told her all this. She listened with a smile. Then she pulled the rebozo from her head. She was still standing. She had her hair cut close to her skull. She looked like a handsome young man with a faint brown sheen to his skin.

"I shall go as a man," she said.

"But how can you just go away from the convent? You're the Mother Superior."

"I left a note saying I had urgent business with the bishop in Mexico City, and that I would be gone a month. I have left before on similar urgent business. I appointed Sister Caridad in my place. She has no curiosity whatsoever. So do not trouble yourself, señor. I must have men's clothes to travel, *verdad?* What do you think?"

"But I have no money," Slocum replied.

"I will take care of all expenses, señor. It *is* Church business. I want to bring back the treasure of the Virgin." She tossed a leather purse on the bed. It was full of twenty-peso gold pieces. "Clothes, a horse for me, lodging," she said crisply.

"All right," Slocum said. He started to smile. The whole project looked more interesting than hanging out with some unwashed rustlers. And the way she had organized things so efficiently amused him. He liked the idea that she would pay all their expenses, not knowing that he planned to remove the treasure from her when they found it.

"So," she said, "it will be good to start at the market before sunrise. You will buy all the clothes I need, then bring them here. I will dress and we will leave. But you must hurry. Sunrise will be in about half an hour."

"The maid will come in very early with my washed clothes."

"I will be in your bed. She will think I am a whore you took back with you."

Slocum laughed, admiring her bluntness.

"Now, go to the market," she ordered.

"There is no way I can buy clothes for you till I see your body."

She had not considered this. She flushed. "Yes," she said finally, "that is true."

It was no time for false modesty. She stripped off her dress. Underneath she wore only a coarse white cotton undergarment with a severe high neck. It fitted her tightly. She had a ripe body with full, hard breasts. She was long-legged, unusual for an Apache woman. Her hips were a trifle wider than a man's, but not so much wider that they would attract attention. With her short hair and pants and a shirt worn somewhat loose she would pass for a man as long as she remained silent.

He felt the beginnings of an erection. He had better get out fast.

She flushed. Slocum shrugged with a smile that indicated it was an unfortunate situation, but necessary.

Finally she folded her arms. No man had ever seen her this way except Father Gregorio in her childhood. She asked angrily, "Are you done, señor?"

"For now, Pilar. And from now on, call me John."

He went out of the room. She noticed that he moved as swiftly and smoothly as the *tigre* that roamed the *sierra*. Although she was exhausted, she was excited with the adventure, sleeping in a man's bed, a man to whom she was going to entrust her life and honor. Yet she felt a serene confidence. It was probably, she thought, because it had been another man, all those years ago, who had saved her life. She fell asleep.

Five minutes later the maid entered with Slocum's freshly ironed clothes piled on her arm. She closed the door, placed the clothes on a chair, and then pulled off her dress. Underneath, in preparation, she was naked. She lifted the sheet that covered the sleeping Pilar, slid in beside her, and waited patiently for the handsome *gringo* to wake up.

When Slocum opened the door ten minutes later the maid

sat erect in astonishment. She pulled the sheet off Pilar's head and screamed *"Puta!"*

Slocum wasted no time arguing or explaing. He picked up the maid's dress, slapped it over her arm, placed five silver pesos in her right palm, and pushed her into the corridor and closed the door. Pilar had pulled the sheet up to her chin and was breathing quickly.

"Get dressed before any more excitement starts," Slocum said.

He turned his back while she pulled off her undergarment and put on the shorts, shirt, socks, trousers, and boots of a vaquero.

"Do the boots fit?" he asked.

"Yes."

A thought suddenly occurred to him. "Pilar, do you ride?" he asked.

"Father Gregorio put me on a horse as soon as I could hold on to the saddle horn."

"Good. I'll buy a horse for you." He looked at her breasts. "Here's a jacket. Wear it loose all the time." He tossed it to her and she put it on. "Good," he said. "And now choose a name for yourself."

"Rosario."

"Fine." They walked quietly down the corridor, but in the front entrance to the *posada* they came across the maid busily scrubbing the floor. She looked up and when she saw Pilar a sly smile appeared.

"Buenas dias, maricón," she said, and spat on the floor.

Slocum had to explain the word to Pilar as they walked to the livery stable. She wobbled in the unaccustomed boots. She flushed violently when Slocum finished.

Then she heaved a deep sigh and crossed herself. It was going to be an interesting trip, Slocum thought.

5

Two dirty, dusty, unshaven men sat around a small fire in which four running irons were slowly turning to a cherry red. A third man with a Winchester scanned the horizon from a low, juniper-studded rise nearby. The two men at the fire were Lewis Choate and Emmett Lamb. The man on lookout was named Chris Evans.

Choate and Lamb were from northern Kansas. Evans came from Ohio. They were rustlers. Choate, the leader, was a deceptively mild-looking man. His right ear had been bitten off in a cowtown brawl. Lamb was a lean, rangy man with long yellow teeth. He had big ears with hair growing out of them. He was part Cherokee and ashamed of it. He usually rode round-shouldered to minimize his height.

The spread was owned by Agustin Aguilar. He ran four

thousand head of fine stock on his ranch. It spread across rich grazing land not far from Our Lady of the Rivers. Aguilar's men were noted for hanging anyone found on the ranch with a running iron in his possession.

None of the three men were happy with this. They could handle about fifty head, trail them to the corral and loading chute at Benson. But they were working with a crooked cattle buyer. This man had to put the cattle on a train that would make a special night stop without any onlookers. That meant a lot of payoffs, so he was offering only half the usual price for prime beef. No matter what the cattle would bring on the legitimate market, he would only give twenty dollars per cow.

"Split a thousand bucks three ways?" Emmett Lamb had said angrily when Choate told him. "Jesus Christ, Lewis! An' them Aguilar vaqueros play rough. We been hangin' 'roun' with you for three months an' you ain't pulled off anythin' worth a damn!"

"True," Evans said. He was the quiet one. Alcohol—even one drink—turned him into a crazed murderer who could only be controlled by Choate. Choate had made it clear that he, Choate, would kill Evans as quick as he would stomp a scorpion under his boot heel if Evans began to move in that direction. Sober, Evans was a fine shot, amiable and easygoing. But he knew that Choate was an even finer shot.

"I keep looking," Choate said calmly.

"Yeah, sure," Lamb said.

"And I found something."

"Somethin' nice?" Lamb asked skeptically.

"I would say so, yes."

"Like the Cattlemen's Bank?"

Evans and Lamb grinned. Choate had lined up the Cattlemen's Bank in Tucson for a busy Friday afternoon when it would have about $75,000 in bank notes ready to be drawn by local ranchers to pay off their hands.

The three men drifted into the bank. Each got into a separate line. Their pretext, if asked, was that they wanted silver dollars in order to trade with the Papagoes, who, like most Indians, would not accept paper money.

Then Choate, who was very observant, caught sight of the five deputies waiting inside the manager's office as that gentleman stepped out. The door was open only for half a second. It was enough. They grimly bought their silver dollars and emerged with their pants pockets bulging.

When they had ridden away side by side, silently cursing, Choate said, "All right. Which one of you two blabbed?"

Both men denied it. Ever since then their luck got worse and worse. Now they had been reduced to risking a necktie party for a lousy three hundred dollars each.

Choate had registered his own brand in Flagstaff, a simple Bar X. He cleverly made no attempt to alter Aguilar's Three Crosses, the same three crosses adopted by the great Hernán Cortés as his. Choate was too smart for that. His story was that he had bought the cattle openly from Aguilar, slapped his road brand on them, and was taking them north. In preparation for this he had had a Mexican write out a receipt in Spanish for the fifty head. It was the kind of thing he had never tried before, and for that reason it would very likely be successful.

Now, although Evans was lookout, he suddenly stood up, mounted, and cantered down to the fire. It was hot and smokeless, made with dried cow chips.

"What the hell are you down here for?" demanded Choate, annoyed.

"I'll tell you why, Choate. I just don't feel lucky. An'

that's the truth. I don't like the feel of this. What I want is to drop the dang thing we got here an' lissen to that other nice thing you found for us."

"Me too," Lamb said. He stood up and dropped his running iron back into the fire.

"You want to drop three hundred bucks? Just like that?"

"Just like that," Evans said amiably. He bent down, grabbed the four running irons, and slung them as hard as he could into a deep arroyo fifty feet away. "Believe me?"

"Well, hell, Chris," Choate said slowly, "I guess I got to."

He sat down cross-legged and sighed.

"So what's the deal?"

"Let's set awhile." The three men unsaddled their horses, which they had kept ready to move fast if they had to. Choate filled a battered white enamel coffeepot with water from the narrow creek that trickled at the bottom of the nearby arroyo. The four running irons had slipped between some high-narrow boulders. He climbed up again. They were sitting with their backs against their saddles when seven horsemen suddenly appeared on the hill where Evans had been lookout. The horses trotted purposefully towards them. The lead rider reined in.

"*Buenos dias,*" he said.

"Who the hell are you?" Choate asked. He knew very well that it was Agustin Aguilar's *mayor-domo*.

"I? I work for Aguilar," the man said. "You are on our ranch, trespassing, no? You mind if we look around a little?"

"Shit, no," Choate said with a grin. Three horsemen began to ride in and out of the nearby grazing cattle, looking for a freshly blotted brand. Three men were watching Choate and his two men with their hands on their gun butts. The *mayor-domo* wandered about, very obviously looking for running irons. The three riders came back and shook their heads.

The *mayor-domo* mounted. "You are welcome to cross this ranch. But not to stay on it."

"Let me kill the fucker," Evans whispered in Choate's left ear.

With a wide smile, Choate said gently, "Saddle up, you dumb son of a bitch. You saved our lives by dumping those irons. You pull on him now and we're all dead." Evans hesitated. Then he turned and slung the saddle blanket onto his horse. Lamb followed his lead.

"We'll be moseying along," Choate told the *mayor-domo*. "On Christian spreads we'd be invited for supper. Not here, I guess."

The *mayor-domo's* face was frozen. He said nothing. He watched Choate saddle up. Then the three Americans rode south. At the crest of the first low ridge they turned back to look. The vaqueros stood motionless facing them.

"Jesus," Lamb said, "that's what I'd call *close*."

They turned and began riding away.

Evans said, after a few minutes, "Let's hear your idea. If it ain't a real good one I'm ridin' away from you, Choate."

"Me too," Lamb said.

"All right," Choate said calmly. "I know where there's treasure. Close by."

"Aw, horse turds," Lamb said.

Choate looked at him.

Lamb said, "I heard all them buried treasure stories. Christ almighty, you found the Lost Dutchman? You got one of them old pirate maps made outta parchment? This is the end of the road for me, Choate. Been nice knowin' you. Coming, Chris?"

Evans sighed. "Guess I better. G'bye, Choate."

Choate spurred in front of them, then turned his horse to block them.

"Listen for one minute. Then you can go."

"Oh, why the hell not?" Evans said agreeably. "I need a good laugh."

Choate said, "The Mexicans around here say the old mission—the one on the other side of Baboquivari Peak—used to be full of gold candlesticks. Big ones, pure gold. And that the statue of the Virgin in the chapel had a dress covered solid with diamonds and emeralds and rubies. Big ones."

"Yeah," Lamb said. "Nuestra Señora de los Rios. All fallen down now. Rode by it once."

"The Apache raids were so bad the Papagoes and the Pimas lit out. The priest lit out too, for Chihuahua."

"Well?"

"He took off one night on a mule. A couple days later people around Sasabe saw him riding south."

"Well?"

"Stop talking and listen, damn it. When he went by Sasabe he was riding light. No saddlebags, *nothing.*"

Evans, who was not too smart, said impatiently, "So what, for Christ's sake?"

Choate said, "So he must have hidden the treasure close to the mission."

Lamb said, baring his yellow teeth like a wolf's, "Yes. And so what do we do, go down to Chihuahua an' hold his feet over a fire till he talks?"

"Why, no," Choate said gently. "Oh, no. We hold his feet over a fire at Nuestra Señora de los Rios."

About three days before Choate had this conversation with Lamb and Evans, three men named Harry Mead, Sam Hart, and George Clay were shoving thirty-five Mormon horses into a corral at Mezquital, in Sonora. Mezquital was on the road that ran from Hermosillo through Magdalena and across the Arizona border.

They were Mormon horses because they had been Mormon property three days before. The Mexican government had permitted the Mormons to establish ranches on the upper Magdalena River after they had been run out of Utah for their custom of having multiple wives. The Mormons would never start a revolution. They kept to themselves, promised not to proselytize, and did not object too much to taxation.

The three men were in their mid-forties. They had all originated in southern Kansas. All had ridden with Quantrill. When the Civil War was over they knew there were too many people who wanted to settle old scores. So they rode away after Appomattox. Since they worked well together as a team, they kept doing it all over the West. They were cruel men. None of them had any property or money to show for all the murders, rapes, and robberies they had committed. They were beginning to yearn for some sort of security.

They hated Northerners. That was one reason why they had taken such pleasure in stealing the Mormon horses. The Mexican horse trader, a man named Lorenzo Muñoz, had arranged for this purchase. He knew that the government would look lightly upon any theft by Americans from Americans. Nor would any Mexican who wanted one of those horses give a damn as to its origin.

The three men drove the horses into the corral while Muñoz sat on the top rail and counted.

"Treinta cinco, amigos mios," he said. "All good horses, as you promised. Sixty American dollars each—that is two thousand dollars."

"Twenty-*one* hundred, *amigo*," Harry Mead said. He had little black button eyes sunk deep in his skull.

"I give you American gold double eagles, one hundred of them. Surely you will not object, especially since there is a little problem about your not having a bill of sale?"

Harry closed his eyes. He always did this before he went into violent action. He was only five feet six and weighed a hundred and fifty-five pounds. George Clay and Sam Hart had seen him do that before he moved against men weighing over two hundred. And when he had them down he jumped up and down on their faces with his boots. That over, he deliberately raked them across the eyes with his big Mexican spurs.

Muñoz was not stupid. When Hart and Clay moved back to give Mead room, Muñoz suddenly realized he could be in for a rough time. Usually, this far inside Mexico—Mezquital was eighty miles below the border—Americans tended to be cautious about starting trouble. Mexican jails were bad and especially so for Americans, who had no friends or relatives to bring them food. And in Mexico no prisoners were fed by the jail authorities.

But these three, he knew immediately, would not hesitate to shoot. They had the look of dogs with rabies. They would shoot to kill, and very efficiently, Muñoz felt. He felt a little tremor of fear. When they had shot him and taken the money, they would ride very calmly to Arizona and just as efficiently kill anyone who tried to stop them. Muñoz felt that even any Apache war party trying to lift their scalps would be very sorry.

So he sighed, reached into his pocket, and added five more double eagles to the five little piles he had stacked on the top railing. Mead counted out the gold and silently handed his men their share.

"Any time, any time," Muñoz said. The three men paid him no attention. They turned away just as Slocum and Pilar rode up. Harry Mead, very perceptive, stared at her. There was something about the slender rider that was not quite right. He couldn't put his finger on it yet. But he would. He knew he would.

6

Pilar's horse had sprained its shoulder in a bad fall that morning. When they rode into Mezquital, Slocum asked for a horse trader with fair prices and was directed to Muñoz.

Pilar dismounted. Harry Mead, half a block away, turned in his saddle to watch. It was a fateful turn; many things happened as a result.

Because—and this was unusual—Slocum pulled off the saddle for the young fellow. He slung it over the corral rail. And the young fellow—as Mead noticed—did not seem to have a broken arm or anything like that, which could explain this behavior on the bigger man's part. The young fellow pulled off his saddle blanket all right, then took off the bridle and bit without any awkward arm movements. Mead found this very curious.

"You fellers go to the *Flor de Sonora,*" he said suddenly. "I got somethin' to do."

41

He did the thinking for the group. Since they wanted to drink they rode off cheerfully to the *cantina*, which lay on the main road to Arizona.

Mead rode past Muñoz's corral casually and slowly. The taller, older man was now talking to Muñoz, who was exhibiting Mead's Mormon horses. The tall man nodded and opened the corral gate. He walked among the nervous horses while he examined them carefully. It was obvious to Mead that the man was an expert. He unerringly went to the gray sorrel Mead had considered taking for himself. He opened the horse's mouth, then lifted and checked the hooves. The sorrel was restless, but the stranger soothed it easily.

The man then turned to Muñoz. They were obviously discussing price. Finally, the man pointed to the horse that the slender person had ridden. Muñoz, who was quite fat, heaved himself across to the horse, looked at the sprained shoulder, then nodded. A trade had been arranged. The big man gave some money to Muñoz, signaled to his partner, who pulled the saddle blanket from the top rail, and then lifted arms to throw it over the Mormon horse.

It was then that Mead finally understood why the younger person had received such consideration from the older man. It was clearly a woman, and a very attractive one at that.

This interested Mead. They were travelers, and had come some distance from the south. They were heading north, Mead's direction. And Mead's favorite relaxation was rape. This was one reason why he could never return to Kansas. He would be shot on sight, even though twenty years had passed since he begun bothering the wives and daughters of Northern sympathizers.

What could two people—and one of them a woman—do against *three* Quantrill veterans?

Mead went to get his men. He would trail the strange

couple and catch them the same night, or the next night.
He was in no hurry. The suspense would be pleasurable.
Afterwards, as was his habit, he would kill the woman.

"I don't see no one," Evans said. "Place looks deserted.
Like a ghost mission." He laughed at his feeble joke.

Choate did not look at him, but slid off his horse and
dropped the reins. Nothing stirred at Nuestra Señora de los
Rios except birds hunting insects in the tall grass.

Sweat made their dirty shirts stick to their bodies. Fur-
nace-hot winds blew from the Sonora desert. The men were
broke, hungry, and angry at their poor luck.

"Hey, there's a couple chickens down there!" Lamb said.
"An' tomatoes! Let's cook us a couple them chickens an'
pick a bushel them tomatoes!"

He and Evans let out a yell and rode hard down the slope.
They splashed across the shallow river as fast as they could
go.

Choate followed slowly, his eyes probing everywhere.
If the old priest were not there, this trip would be the end
of his little band. They had worked well together and he
would regret losing them.

The other two had dismounted and were busy chasing
the squawking chickens in the garden. The chickens were
not used to people. They fluttered away, then took flight
and landed on the low branch of a peach tree, then jumped
off as Evans came near, and proved so agile that neither
Evans nor Lamb could come near them.

Their failure made them mean. Evans pulled his Colt
and let off a snap shot. It almost blew apart one chicken.

The explosion woke Father Gregorio. He leaned on one
elbow on the stone floor inside the chapel. He struggled
painfully to his feet and reached for the crude cane he had

fashioned for himself soon after Slocum had left to find Pilar.

He moved slowly to the door of the chapel and raised a hand to shadow his eyes against the harsh light.

Lamb was looking at the remains of the chicken. "Aw, Chris," he said, "all you left us are the legs. That's damn poor shootin', boy."

Evans said in his sullen way, "You ain't gonna do no better, Emmett."

"Watch, sonny. Just watch." Lamb drew his Colt, took a wide-legged stance, aimed at a chicken roosting in the peach tree, and fired. Just as he squeezed the trigger the chicken flew off.

Evans let out a burst of laughter. Choate knew that the men would soon be hard to handle. He turned to walk into the chapel and the first thing he saw was a very old man wearing a brown robe standing in the doorway.

"Padre Gregorio?" Choate asked softly.

"*Sí. Bienvenido a Nuestra Señora de los Ríos.*"

"Anyone else here?" Choate said in English.

Father Gregorio understood English, but he replied in Spanish, "All have abandoned this place except God and this poor sinner—and the Virgin herself."

"Ah," Choate said. He understood Spanish. He was suddenly jubilant. He felt sure things would work out. He said in Spanish, "I want to ask a few questions, Father."

"I can offer you only dried peaches and tomatoes, my son. The chickens are for eggs. But you will have to pick the tomatoes yourselves. I am too weak to offer hospitality."

"I have something else in mind, Father." He noticed that the old man was leaning with all his weight on the cane. To save time and show that he meant business, Choate kicked the cane away. As the old man fell, an amazed expression came over his face.

"Make a fire," Choate said. He bent down and ripped the hem of the old priest's robe. The fabric was so old that it tore easily. One never knew—the old man's screams might attract attention from someone riding by.

Choate tore off a small piece, thrust it into the priest's mouth, and used the remainder to bind the gag firmly into place. Choate did everything well. That was why Lamb and Evans had stuck with him as long as they had. Lamb went outside and took a length of rawhide from his saddlebag. With it he tied the old man's wrists together. They looked as fragile as chicken bones.

Then they went to work.

7

Slocum had bought the grey sorrel from Muñoz about three in the afternoon. By eight that evening he and Pilar had ridden thirty miles north along the beaches bordering the Rio Magdalena. He had decided that it would be too risky staying in *posadas*. Any sharp-eyed person might be curious about the slender, good-looking Indian youth with new clothes who rode as if he had not ridden for years. Pilar's thigh muscles had not yet adjusted to riding. When she dismounted she walked painfully.

So they slept in the open. He had picked up two blankets and a tarpaulin for her and taught her how to spread the canvas, put the blankets on top, bring up the bottom end of the tarp over the blankets, then flip over each side of the tarp. There she had it—a warm bedroll. If it rained, all she had to do was reach up and pull the top end of the tarp over her head.

He felt a lot of sexual tension, but did his best to keep it at a minimum. His code of honor did not permit him to make a move toward a nun. As for Pilar, she knew that all nuns, especially when young, did feel sexual desire. The point was to change it into love for humanity and Jesus Christ. Since she had never experienced sex, it was not too difficult for her. But once, when Slocum had scouted the terrain on both sides of a clear blue little lake and seen no signs of human presence anywhere, he told her he was going to bathe.

She turned her back. He stripped, washed his under-clothes and socks with the bar of brown laundry soap he carried with him, and draped them over a manzanita to dry. Then he stepped naked into the lake and immediately stepped on a sharp stone.

"God dam it to hell!" he swore, and the startled Pilar turned. Before she realized it was not serious, she had seen his wide shoulders and narrow hips, and the various pale scars scattered over his body. His back was to her, so she had not seen his genitals, but she imagined how he must look. Her face flushed. She said a silent prayer as contrition. But she did not know if that did any good for she still felt a rush of excited interest.

When he had changed and told her it was her turn to wash her clothes and bathe, he made a firm resolve to keep a sharp lookout to avoid any surprises from any unfriendly folk—either Apache or Mexican. Still, he turned to look at her after she had waded in as far as her knees. She was unusually tall for an Apache woman, with long, slender legs and melon-heavy breasts with cherry-sized nipples. It was the kind of woman's body that Slocum most admired. She bent down to scoop up some water in her cupped palms and her breasts swung free. Slocum felt a stiffening in his groin.

He did not worry about her noticing it, because he was fully dressed now. But when she had dressed and come up from the lake and began to gather odd bits of dried wood to make their supper fire, she saw the bulge in his pants.

She averted her eyes and they ate in silence. Slocum thought how glad he'd be when all this would be over and done with, when he could go into a cowtown whorehouse, pick a woman who attracted him, and then screw her without any embarrassment. She'd pull her dress over her head, pull off her camisole—if she wore anything at all—and that would be that.

Just thinking about that gave him an even larger erection. He was grateful for the deepening darkness. "I'll take the first two-hour watch," he told her, and she fell asleep immediately in her bedroll. This trip could not end fast enough for him. When the stars had shifted the right distance, he woke her up.

"See up there?" he told her. "When that star moves to that position, wake me up."

"Did you ever own a watch?" she asked, sitting up and yawning.

"Not necessary on a clear night."

Like most cowmen who lived in the open and watched the sky continually because they needed information about snow or rain, he could judge time within a fifteen-minute span.

He handed her his Colt. "You see anything suspicious," he told her, "call out *'Quien es?'* If you don't get an answer, fire one shot straight up. That'll wake me."

Nothing happened. The fire went out. He slept.

But Harry Mead, two miles back, had seen the fire. Satisfied that they were going to sleep, he rode down the ridge. Hart and Clay were scooping cold beans into their mouths. Mead had ordered no fires.

"I'm awful hongry," Sam Hart said sourly. "Eatin' beans for two days is awful. Next steak I see I'll fall on it like the hull dang Missouri on a sandbar, see effen I don't."

"Soon, soon," Mead said. The man who was riding with the woman looked hard and competent. At each ridge the man had stopped, pivoted in the saddle, and looked in every direction. If they attacked too soon, someone would be hurt, or even killed. That price would be too high just to have the woman.

But Mead knew a trick or two, due to his long years of guerrilla fighting and the subsequent years on the Indian frontier.

Every time he came near a ridge or a curve in the road, he halted. He crept forward on his belly and very carefully peered over the crest or around the curve until he saw Slocum disappear. Then he moved to the next ridge with his men. Soon enough, Mead knew he would think of a way to get rid of the tall rider. Then he would have the woman at his mercy. When he was finished the other two could have her. Then he would kill her. It would be the way it had always been.

Next morning Pilar said, "I'm used to riding now. It doesn't hurt any more. Can we go faster? I'm very anxious about Father Gregorio."

"You think you can handle a hard ride?" Slocum asked.

"Yes."

Slocum had a fine horse and Muñoz's gray sorrel could keep up with his. A day's hard riding, say a day and a half, and they would reach the mission. Both horses were in top condition. Water and forage were in good supply.

"Porque no?" he said.

They easily outdistanced the three pursuers. Mead was angry. He should have attacked the night before, he now realized. But then he became intrigued about their increased speed. Why should two riders, one a woman dressed as a man, suddenly begin to move fast? Mead was sure they hadn't been spotted; he had a fine instinct for these things.

Since one direction was as good as another for three gentlemen in their aimless profession, he shrugged and decided to keep following them. They would be easy to track. But there was no way the three Kansans could keep up Slocum's pace with their own second-rate horses.

"Stop moanin'," he told his men. "We'll eat hot food tonight." Near Carrizal he bought some mutton chops from a sheepherder, rejecting Evans's offer to kill the greaser. They broiled them skewered on a sharp stick. Then the men fell asleep while Mead, with his hands clasped behind his head, wondered once more why the two strangers were hurrying north.

8

Choate couldn't get anything useful out of Father Gregorio even when the old priest's flesh had reddened, blistered, then charred to black.

"Tell me where you put the candlesticks," he asked again and again.

But the old priest kept saying, *"No me recuerdo, no me recuerdo!"*

"He forgets," Choate said in a disgusted tone. He resumed his hot work. But it was true; Father Gregorio's memory had faded with age. He simply no longer remembered where he had hidden the treasure.

"It was so long ago!" he screamed.

Evans asked, "What's he sayin' now?"

"Says it happened long ago." Choate stood up and shoved his hands in his back pockets and stared at the contorted, sweating face of the old priest.

"I tell you two things, Choate," Lamb said. "One is, I bet he's tellin' the truth. Gawd, look how old he is! An' two is, this is the last straw. I'm shovin' off. Comin', Chris?"

"Yeah, guess so."

"An' we don't want you ridin' with us, neither. You brought us nothin' but bad luck, Choate." Choate watched them mount and ride away. He said nothing. Behind him Father Gregorio groaned in agony and died, but Choate did not see this.

"Shit," Choate said wearily. He mounted and rode slowly after the two men. Maybe they would cool off soon. By then he should have another plan ready. His mind set to work and he began to examine all the possibilities.

At eleven o'clock the next morning Slocum and Pilar reined in at the top of the ridge which stretched along the southern side of the broad, grassy meadows which long ago had been farmed by the Papagoes for the glory of Nuestra Señora de los Rios.

Pilar had been tense and restless ever since they had risen six hours before. She half stood in her stirrups and stared at the garden far below.

"Look, look!" she cried out happily. "He has kept the weeds out of the garden! He is still alive!" She spurred her Mormon horse and raced down the chaparral-studded hillside.

But Slocum had noticed that several horsemen had ridden through the garden trampling the tomato plants and crushing melons under the horse's hooves. The tracks led out of the garden and then went east. He did not like that. People simply did not ride through a man's garden like that. Not decent people. Slocum did not like the feel of it at all. He rode down to the mission with a sinking sensation in his stomach.

When Slocum reined in in front of the chapel he knew he was right. She had run out and was clutching his stirrup and sobbing hysterically. Then she slipped to the ground, to her knees. She bent over till her forehead touched the ground.

Before Slocum entered the chapel he knew it was going to be bad. The smell of charred human flesh was unmistakeable.

It took him two hours to break open a grave in the hard-packed clay of the mission's cemetery. Father Gregorio had buried many baptized Indians there. Every once in a while someone would ride up with a bunch of desert flowers crammed into a tobacco can or an empty sardine can. These would be placed wordlessly at the base of a decaying wooden cross. The flowers would dry within minutes in the intense heat, the tin would rust away in a year or so, and when the cross finally rotted away it would not be replaced.

Slocum wrapped the frail old body in a blanket. He made sure that the burned feet would not be visible to Pilar. He lowered the amazingly light body into the grave. Then he turned to Pilar and waited for her to say a prayer.

She had not spoken a word since she had seen the body in the chapel. She sat cross-legged against the chapel wall in the style of her Apache ancestors. Her black eyes glittered as she watched Slocum dig.

She shook her head slowly. Slocum shrugged. He faced the grave and recited what he remembered of the Twenty-third Psalm. Then he said, "You were a good man, Father Gregorio. The bastards who did this will pay for it."

He reached for the shovel. When the first lump of clay

hit the blanket she began to moan. Slocum finished. He wondered what kind of men would torture a priest, a harmless old man.

"I want a cross with his name on it," Pilar said.

"It will be done. But first I have some business to take care of. Then I'll come back."

"I'll go with you."

"No." The men who had killed Father Gregorio were less than a day's journey ahead of him. By the way they had ridden out, they were in no hurry. If Slocum rode hard he could catch them at their night camp. He figured from the tracks that there were three of them.

"I want to go with you, John. I want to know why they did it. Only then will I be able to forgive them."

"No."

Slocum filled his canteen at the river. She walked beside him. As he picked a few tomatoes and put them in his saddlebag in order to save water in case the trail took him across a dry stretch, she asked him once more.

"No, Pilar."

She finally accepted his refusal. "And how long will you be gone?"

"One day, maybe two. Stay here. Don't spend the night in the chapel. Don't make a fire. They might circle back. You never know. Sleep on the slope there, under those piñons." He had bought her a Colt and a gunbelt in Mesquital and taught her how to use it.

"If they come back and come near you, wait till they get within ten feet. Hold it with both hands, the way I showed you. Point it at their stomachs and pull the trigger."

"Will they die?" she whispered.

"Yes."

"I do not want to kill anyone."

Slocum said, "You will make that decision at the time. You must remember that these people would kill you without remorse. I advise the same treatment. Goodbye."

She watched him ride away to the east. He was a strange, hard, cruel man, but she liked him.

The dusty trail led east. The three riders had arrived together at the mission. Two had left together, the third man had followed some time after. After a few miles the third man had caught up with the first two and then the three men had ridden together.

Where were they going? It would be helpful to know. People who had done what they had done had probably done things like that before. So, in a sense, they were professionals. They had tried to get information from Father Gregorio—very likely, Slocum thought, the location of the treasure of the Virgin. Clearly they had failed. So they were probably broke.

And three broke professionals were probably heading for a place where they could either steal or borrow money. The only place to the east which filled that bill was Tombstone. One hundred and thirty miles. But they would need food and liquor. Both they could find at the sutler's store at Fort Douglas, thirty-five miles east. They were probably there already. Maybe they would spend the night there. If he made good time, he could catch them in the morning.

He pushed spurs into his horse's belly.

Harry Mead put both hands on his pommel and leaned forward. There were recent tracks into the old mission and recent tracks leading out again. He was not as adept as Slocum in reading sign. He decided to be careful in his approach.

•   •   •

Pilar had paid no attention to Slocum's instructions. She had rolled herself in her blanket and lay down on the chapel floor the way Father Gregorio used to. She tried to sleep, but could not. She dozed briefly, woke up, stared at the ceiling, cried a little, and then tried to sleep again. It was useless. She finally dozed off, but woke at sunrise. She heated some beans and scooped them up with the last of the tortillas they had bought from a Mexican woman the day before at Calabasas. She sat cross-legged under the statue, where the ventilation through the broken windows and front door made a cool draft.

The gun and gunbelt were too heavy to wear. She put them to one side.

Then she foraged around and found a sun-dried board two feet long and six inches wide. She opened a small jackknife Slocum had bought for her in Mezquital and traced Father Gregorio's name on the board. Then it was, for the first time in her life, that she realized she had never known his last name. Tears welled up. She wiped them away with the back of one hand, bent down, and became totally absorbed in carving PADRE GREGORIO.

Mead and his two men rode to the mission. They rode slowly, hands on their gun butts. When they reached it Mead held up a hand and dismounted. He prowled around, saw the recently filled grave, and wondered a bit about that. He decided that some Indian must have buried his dead there, some Christianized Papago, probably. He walked into the chapel warily and the first thing he saw was Pilar, sitting under the statue of the Virgin. She was so absorbed in her carving that she was not aware at first that he was staring at her. It was so hot inside, after the breeze had died down, that she had unbuttoned the top three buttons of her shirt. Since she was bent forward Mead now had absolute proof that the young rider was a woman.

He had only seen one horse outside, the Mormon gray he had sold to Muñoz. It had been hobbled and was browsing in the meadow outside the mission. After he had enjoyed her he would sell the horse once more and make a double profit. He let out a happy sigh.

She jerked her head up.

"Buenas tardes," Mead said with a friendly smile.

She went quickly for the gun. Mead followed her look and stepped in front of it. It was not a gesture that relaxed her. He was still smiling, while he stared at her breasts. She began to button her shirt.

"Too late," Mead said.

Her palm was sweating. She wiped it dry on her pants leg and took a firm grip on the handle of her jackknife.

He stepped in front of her and shook his head gently. He did not like to frighten the game too early. He put his right palm on his gun butt and held out his left hand.

Many things flashed through her mind. None of this man's gestures or expressions gave her confidence. Perhaps he was the same man who had tortured Father Gregorio. If she were to give him the knife, there would go her only defense. She had no idea when Slocum would return. If she gave this smiling man the knife she had no doubt he would rape her. Certainly her vow gave her the right to defend herself if she did not kill; there were some nuns who would not resist at all, and so would resign themselves to God's will. But not her.

Perhaps it was her Apache heritage. Apaches had never surrendered to superior force, not for three hundred years. Perhaps it was in her blood.

"Very well," she said. "Here is the knife." She slashed

a deep cut from the base of his index finger diagonally across his palm to his wrist. She used the element of surprise to step out and reach for her gun. It was a mistake. Slocum would have told her. She was leaving Mead's right hand free in an unimpeded access to his Colt. She should have tried to cut his right wrist and thus rendered his gun hand useless. Then she would have had some chance to get her gun and use it.

So she had lost. She faced him with the small blade of her knife raised, but she was no match for the speed with which Mead pulled his Colt and smashed the barrel against the side of her head. She was unconscious before she reached the floor.

9

It was dark before Slocum reached Fort Douglas. It lay in a broad valley surrounded by the savage, grim peaks of the Chiricahua homeland. From six miles away he had seen the scattered yellow pinpoints at the windows of the fort.

Just outside the fort proper was a collection of ramshackle structures which housed the saloon, the brothel, and the sutler's store. Three saddled horses stood at the hitching rack outside the store. Slocum hitched his horse beside the others and ran his hand over the three horses. All were rested and recently fed and watered.

"Lookin' to buy 'em?"

"Always possible," Slocum said without turning around.

"Wouldn't'cha say it's smarter to look 'em over in daylight?" the voice went on. It had an assured, arrogant quality that irritated Slocum.

"Yep. But I want to get rid of mine fast, and I figured someone with a couple drinks in him might go for a fast trade."

Choate chuckled. "You're honest, stranger. What's wrong with your pony?"

"Nothin' much. Fine in all respects. Except whenever I bend over he bites a chunk outta my ass."

Choate laughed again. "I don't think we'll be sellin' ours. You comin' for a drink?"

"Yeah. But I got to dig out a stone from his left front."

Choate nodded and went back. Slocum bent down and felt each horseshoe of the three horses. He found what he was looking for on the fifth try: a left front shoe had a V-shaped indentation on the lower right edge. It belonged to one of the horses which had carried the three murderers to the mission. A flash of rage shot through him. He took a deep breath and went in.

The place was full of soldiers; payday had been the previous day. Three civilians were sitting at a round table. One looked up at Slocum and said, "This is the feller who's been looking at our horses. My name's Choate. Join us?"

"I like the black. Want to trade?" Slocum asked, with a calm expression. The black had the V-shaped nick.

"Hell, no," Choate said pleasantly. "He's mine. Had him for two years. Follows me around like a puppy, always looking for a lump of sugar. This is Emmett Lamb, and the lanky fellow is Chris Evans."

"Pleased to meet you," Slocum said. "I'm John Slocum." He had decided to use his real name. It was well known along the border.

"Are *you* John Slocum?" Evans asked with interest. "If you're the man who stuck up the Union Pacific on that upgrade at Raton Pass three years ago, I wanna tell you that

was a damn fine job! I heard you got forty-five thousand
in hundred-dollar notes, all old and worn, all diff'rent serial
numbers. An' then you just dropped off the train like a ripe
peach when she was crawlin' along, an' there was your
hoss, all saddled, tied to a tree, an' you rode off slick as a
whistle. That true?"

"Eighty-seven thousand," Slocum said. Slocum had noticed the glances sent toward Choate by the other two men
while Evans recited the train story. Clearly they had been
having some sort of altercation. He decided to pour some
oil on the fire.

"My, my," Lamb said with admiration. "Now that's what
I call *real* plannin'." He stared at Choate, who responded
with an irritated flush.

"Not havin' much luck lately?" Slocum asked casually.

"*Luck?* Lately, if wild geese cost ten cents a dozen we
couldn't buy a hummin'bird's ass. An' that's God's truth."

The use of the word "God" by someone who had tortured
a priest hit Slocum like a bucket of ice water. His face
contorted slightly against his will, and Choate, who was
very observant, noticed this and wondered at it. Slocum
realized his error and recovered by calmly explaining that
he had been brought up in a religious home and still would
not take the name of the Lord in vain.

"I c'n unnerstan' that," Evans said. "Beg your pardon,
John."

Slocum waved a hand to show that all was forgiven.

"I drink, though," he said, and, turning to the sutler,
who was reading a month-old newspaper spread out on the
counter, ordered whisky for all.

"Thanks, John," Choate said. "We're scrapin' the bottom
of the barrel these days."

"We all have our ups and downs," Slocum said with an

understanding smile. What he had to do was separate Choate from the other two men. Choate was a strong, intelligent man. Once he was out of the way, the two followers would be relatively easy to handle.

After Slocum had bought the third round, Evans's tongue began to loosen. He described the rustling fiasco with shouts of angry laughter. He went into great detail about a gold shipment out of Cripple Creek which had to be canceled because a sudden cloudburst had washed out the bridge over which the stagecoach was due to travel. They had waited there for three days, wondering why the goddamn coach hadn't shown up until Choate sent Evans into town to find out what had happened.

"Three days without food!" Lamb snapped, exposing his long yellow teeth. "Jesus Christ Al—oh, excuse me, John."

"That's all right, Emmett."

"An' then this last thing, over at the old mission, what was its name, Chris?"

"Some greaser name."

"Of course it was a greaser name! They're all greaser names down here, you idjit!"

Chris put down his shotglass. Slocum recognized his expression. It was the look on a man's face when he was about to explode and didn't give a damn about the consequences.

Lamb realized he had gone too far. "Sorry, Chris."

Chris's flushed face slowly cleared. He took a deep breath and resumed sipping.

"What happened?" Slocum asked with an air of polite interest.

Lamb began, "Well—"

"I don't think Mr. Slocum wants to hear everything that's happened to us, boys," Choate said pleasantly.

"Why the hell not?" Evans said angrily. "An' I'm not your boy, neither!" He turned to Slocum and jerked a thumb at Choate.

"Choate here heard a story 'bout the old priest at the mission. Seems many years ago the Cherrycahuas here were pawin' the ground fierce. So they was allowed to pull back to Chihuahua. The mission had lots of gold an' jewels an' the old priest hid 'em an' took off. Later he came back. So Choate here figgers—"

Choate's face flushed with rage. He stood up, slammed his glass on the table, and walked out.

"—the old priest knows where it was. So we ride over an' the ol' bastard wouldn't spit out where it was. Another one of Choate's great idees. Shit!"

Slocum signaled for another round.

"Couldn't you persuade him to talk? There are ways." He grinned.

"Sure. We built a fire an' Choate held his feet. The ol' fool still wouldn't talk. So there we were, flat broke. Choate thinks we oughta get a grubstake together by workin' in the mines 'round Tombstone. But I been a miner. That's hard, dangerous work. A man c'n git kilt lickety-split. Mebbe you got some good idees? We like your looks, John."

So all three were responsible for Father Gregorio's death. And Choate was the principal.

"Where'd Choate go?"

"Who the hell—excuse me, John—who knows or gives a shit? He gits up an' walks around by hisself lots of times. 'Thinkin', thinkin',' he says. An' it don' do him no damn good. Look at the three of us! We can't hardly scratch up four bucks among us. If it wasn't fer you comin' along we'd a had one drink apiece tonight."

Slocum nodded. He stood. He walked out into the darkness to the hitching post. There were three dark masses on the ground, still held by their reins to the horizontal rail. Choate had cut the throats of Slocum's horse as well as the horses of Evans and Lamb. The only other horses in the area were those belonging to the cavalry. And no one with any sense stole cavalry horses. There was no way to explain away the big US brand on their left flanks.

Slocum felt a kind of admiration for Choate. He would tell him that when they met again. And they would meet, Slocum promised himself.

He poked his head inside the sutler's store. "Chris, Emmett," he said. "I got something to show you."

"Yeah? What?"

"A goodbye present from Choate," he said.

He stood aside and listened as they cursed in rage, forgetting that Slocum did not like anyone to blaspheme in his presence. *Good, good,* Slocum thought. At least he had driven a wedge between the three of them.

Finally the two men stopped cursing. They understood the problem of stealing cavalry mounts as well as Slocum did. When they tired and slumped down with their backs against the wall of the sutler's store Slocum said mildly, "Evans, you got a rawhide *reata,* don't you?"

"Yeah. Gonna commit suicide?"

"No. We're going to steal three horses from the cavalry corral."

Slocum had decided that the only thing to do was to steal three cavalry mounts. There simply was no other way to get horses in the area of Fort Douglas.

"You ever see the corral?" Lamb asked. "It's got 'dobe walls six feet high, two feet thick, an' an iron gate which is got an iron chain and two padlocks. They don' need no sentries. No one's gonna sneak into *that* place."

It was typical of other army corrals in Apache country.

"Give me your *reata.*"

"I guess you know what you're doin'," Evans said. He bent down and took his *reata* from the dead horse.

At the corral the horses became uneasy as the silent figures neared. They stamped and snorted.

"Emmett, you get inside."

"What the hell for?" Emmett retorted.

"Oh, shit," Slocum said wearily. "*I'll* get inside." He went over the wall in an easy, sinuous move. Once on the other side, he asked Lamb to toss him one end of the *reata.* When it came snaking over the wall he caught it.

"Hold your end tight," Slocum said. He pulled his end hard and the startled Lamb had his knuckles slammed against the adobe.

"Pull back hard," Slocum said softly. "We're going to saw through."

It was an old Apache trick he had seen done once at Fort Davis in the Huachuca Mountains. The rawhide cut through the adobe as if it were some kind of hard butter. In half an hour he and Lamb had sawed two cuts from top to bottom thirty inches apart. Ten minutes more and the horizontal cut which joined them at the bottom had been made.

"Catch the wall," Slocum said. The adobe toppled over and the two men deposited it gently on the ground. By then Slocum had already cut and twisted the *reata* into three hackamores. They took three good mounts and led them outside. Slocum had noticed a bucket hanging from a nail at the water trough nearby. They set the wall back into place. Slocum filled the bucket with water and made a thick paste from the churned-up clay in the corral. With that he sealed up the cuts on both sides. By morning it would be dry and invisible. And no one at the fort would even think the horses had been stolen. The horse wrangler would probably get into trouble for not driving them into the corral the evening before. There wouldn't be any pursuit.

They led the horses back to the store and saddled up. Without a word the two men followed Slocum's lead. They had shifted their allegiance to him without a word being said. Apaches hung about the fort waiting to pick off lone travelers and stragglers, but three well-armed men could travel in perfect safety.

After a few minutes' trotting Lamb said, "That was a pretty smart trick. I wanna throw in with you, Slocum."

"Me, too," Evans said.

The sky was full of stars. There was no moon, but the stars gave some light. "Let's travel a bit," Slocum said. "I want to put distance between us and the fort."

"Whatever you say," Lamb said agreeably.

In an hour Slocum said, "Let's get some sleep." He planned to kill them the next day after explaining exactly why he was doing it.

They turned up into a small arroyo and within minutes found a level stretch. They hobbled the horses and were fast asleep within minutes. Slocum took the first watch. Then he woke Lamb, who protested, "We're safe here."

"Two hours," Slocum said, unmoved. It was an hour from sunrise. He saddled his horse.

"What's up?" Lamb asked.

"I want to see if I can find any sign of Choate."

"Kill the son of a bitch," Lamb said with heat. He settled back against his saddle and folded his arms.

Slocum watered his horse at a small trickle that ran through the bottom of the arroyo. The light grew stronger. He found an old bear trail that ran at an angle up through the piñon pine country. Like all animal trails, the path took the easiest way. In half an hour he had reached the ridge top.

He could see for miles in all directions. The sun was up. Dry water courses, tawny brown mountains that had the smooth, sleek look of mountain lions, hazy blue mountains to the east out of which came the Chiricahua Apaches who had driven the Spaniards back to Mexico. Fifteen miles to the east was Fort Douglas. He turned slowly. Far to the west was a tiny black speck moving westward. It might be Choate. A fast ride might let Slocum catch up before sunset. It was worth a try.

He started down for the camp. Before he got close he sensed something wrong. The two horses were gone. So they had left; they had changed their minds about throwing in with him.

It meant he would be chasing three men all over again. He cursed silently. But when he came close he saw something which made him pull his Winchester from its saddle scabbard and hit the ground in one fast movement.

Lamb and Evans were still in their blankets. Sticking up from each motionless body was a cluster of Apache war arrows. Their guns were gone. Slocum wormed closer. The ground was covered with the moccasin prints of two men.

So all was clear. Lamb had just gone to sleep instead of staying on lookout. The Apaches had found them asleep. Each Apache got three arrows ready, stood over Lamb and Evans, and shot three arrows into each man in as many seconds. Then they caught the horses, saddled them, and rode away.

One Apache had hung up his moccasins in a manzanita nearby. He said, as plainly as in a written message, *Thanks for the boots; you can have these useless things.* Slocum stuffed the moccasins in his saddlebag. A man never knew when they might come in handy.

For Slocum there was one consolation: if the two men hadn't decided to ride with him, they might still be alive. Feeling better, he headed for Nuestra Señora de los Rios. Choate could wait. Trails always crossed, sooner or later.

10

Something kept bothering Choate about Father Gregorio. Choate finally believed that the old man was telling the truth when he said he had forgotten where he had put the treasure. But after they had finished with Father Gregorio and had ridden away, Choate kept thinking about the old priest.

And it was this: a man who had forgotten something, and who kept thinking about it, was very likely to fish up that memory suddenly. The mind worked away tirelessly, like a machine, and all of a sudden the answer popped into his mind.

So Choate decided to go back and see if the old man had been working on that problem. He did not know that Father Gregorio had died.

He liked the idea that he was alone now. If those two bastards had lost their faith in his leadership, not only did they deserve to be set afoot in Indian country, but they also deserved to lose their share of the treasure. For Choate was convinced that the treasure was near the mission. He had heard enough fake buried treasure and lost gold stories in his time. He could smell out the ones that gave off a bad stink. This one gave off the correct aroma. He had nothing to lose by going back. At least there was water, grass for his horse, chickens, and tomatoes in the garden. A couple of days there wouldn't hurt.

Then he thought about the expressions on their faces back at Fort Douglas when they stepped outside and saw their dead horses. He wished he could have been there to watch them scream and running around in circles figuring how the hell they could get horses out there, in a place where there were no horses to buy and where the cavalry mounts were so well guarded.

Choate's horse was a four-year-old roan. It stood one hand taller than the usual range pony. It was not a finicky eater, had plenty of endurance, and could forage pretty well on cottonwood leaves if it had to. So he made good time moving at a fast trot.

Late that afternoon he came to Nuestra Señora de los Rios. He reined in. There were four horses in the corral. He had not figured on the old priest having company. If he walked in the old man would single him out. He sat despondently for a few minutes as he tried to figure out his next move.

Then he saw the newly filled grave in the cemetery beside the chapel. His first reaction was relief. No one would recognize him. His second reaction was regret. If they had only taken it easier on the old priest, he'd still be alive, and Choate would have one more chance at the treasure. And his third reaction was still more relief. Now he could ride down and make himself something to eat from the garden. He hadn't eaten in twenty-four hours.

Harry Mead watched Choate through the broken window of the chapel.

"We got a visitor, looks like," he said.

His voice was flat. His left palm was wrapped in a bandage he had torn from Pilar's shirt. It would heal faster if he could reach a doctor who could stitch it up, but the nearest one was two days' ride to the northeast. The hand throbbed painfully.

Pilar sat on the stone floor. Her wrists were tied behind her. The contraction of her shoulder blades thrust her breasts forward. Mead had buttoned the top three buttons of her shirt himself. He did not want to be aroused until he could screw her, and that he would not do if she were unconscious or in pain. This was a matter of principle with Mead. He wanted his victims to know exactly what was happening to them; he wanted the pain to come from his savage thrusts. He liked them to scream with agony.

She had lain inert for several hours after he had pistol-whipped her. When she finally opened her eyes early that morning, they did not focus. It was obvious she had suffered a mild concussion. Mead was annoyed. He would give her another twenty-four hours. If she had not returned by then to full consciousness, Clay and Hart could have her.

"He alone?" Clay asked.

"Yeah," Mead said.

"We c'n handle 'im. How's your hand?"

"Guess, you damn fool!"

"C'mon, George," Hart said shortly. "That hand gives 'im conniption fits." He picked up a Winchester carbine that was standing in a corner of the chapel and cradled it in the crook of his right elbow. He went out first and stood at the edge of the garden, next to a corner of the corral. It was a natural place for the strange rider to aim for.

Sam Hart sat on the ground with his back against a peach-tree trunk. He was in dappled shadow and with his outline thus broken he would be hard to see unless the viewer knew he was there. A man standing in the full glare of the sun couldn't see well into shadow. It was a good flanking position, and if the stranger suddenly were to pull on Clay, a shot from Hart's .30-.30 would take care of him. They had used this bit of strategy frequently and it had never failed.

Choate rode up to Clay. He lifted his right hand and said with a smile, "Afternoon."

Clay nodded. His eyes were cold. Choate knew a professional when he saw one. He looked around casually and spotted the flank man immediately.

"I come in peace, brother," Choate said with a grin.

Clay said suspiciously, "What the hell you talkin' about, mister?"

Mead stepped out of the chapel. "By damn," he said, "I think I reckernize you. You're Lewis Choate. From up 'round Topeka. Am I right?"

"You sure as hell are," Choate said. He stared at Mead. "We ever meet before?"

"We was always missin' one another in those days," Mead said. "Been fifteen years, more or less, I reckon."

Quantrill's men had roamed across eastern Kansas during the War, raping and looting helpless Northern sympathizers. They tended to avoid clashes with any heavily armed group and would have nothing to do with any Northern army unit.

"More or less," Choate said with a smile. He hated Quantrill's men. Several of his relatives had been wounded or killed by them. But he was adept in concealing his emotions.

If he found a project to work on he needed an experienced group. And one thing was sure: anyone who had ridden with Quantrill would be perfect for him.

"Yeah, more or less," Mead mimicked. He still hated Yankees. The Yankees now controlled Kansas and Mead knew he could never go back.

Choate kept smiling. He behaved as if Mead had not made fun of him. Mead's reputation was that he was a killer who frequently flew into a murderous rage on the slightest provocation. He had killed bank tellers who had handed over all the money in their cash drawers, just like that. Choate knew he would have to step warily here.

"Passin' through?" Mead asked. He waved his hand at Hart, who relaxed.

Choate wondered why this group was at the mission. Were they passing through? Or did they have a reason for coming here? Was it for the same reason he was here? Maybe the answer might give him a lever by which he could insert himself into the group, and possibly take command. It was worth a try. He was broke and had nothing to lose.

When Mead waved his hand at Hart a pang of agony shot through it. He winced.

Choate saw a chance to show friendly concern. "Nothing serious, I hope," he said, nodding toward the hand.

"Nope."

"A girl done it!" Hart said, and burst into laughter.

Clay joined in. Then he said, "Yeah, we all thought she was a man at first. Short hair, man's outfit. She's inside waitin' fer Harry to figger out what's next."

Sam Hart added, "Good-lookin' squaw. 'Pache. I got no objection if you git in line. Harry's first, though. Allus has been. Then me. Then George. Wanna look at 'er?"

Choate walked in, more out of curiosity than anything

else. Rape was not in his line. While the others were making remarks about her fine body, Choate was staring at the board she had begun to carve. PADRE GREGORIO, said the outlined letters. He tried to remember the details of the legend. There had been something about an abandoned Apache baby girl the old priest had rescued, then later sent to a convent in Hermosillo. Could this be the girl? Had she come back?

And if so, why had she returned? Choate's intelligent mind quickly found the answer: *She had come to pick up the treasure.*

"Pretty, ain't she?" Hart said. "Trouble is, Harry's gonna kill 'er right afterwards."

"He's *what?*"

"Gonna kill 'er," Hart said placidly. "He allus does that."

Mead looked down at the blood-matted black hair. She was moaning.

"Comin' to," Hart said with satisfaction. "Harry likes 'em live an' kickin'." He wiggled his hips. "Like a trout on a hook, floppin' all over. More excitin'."

Choate knew that the chances of his getting the drop on the three Quantrill men, killing them, and then having the Apache woman to torture for the answer to the treasure's location was small indeed. The men would be vigilant and merciless. A failed murder attempt would be dealt with brutally.

It was best to ask them in, or the woman would be killed and with her would go his last chance at the treasure.

Of course, there was always the strong probability that if they did find the treasure, Mead and his men would kill him. It would be very likely, indeed, since, after all, they had been on opposing sides in the War. Choate sighed. Maybe he could find a couple of good gunfighters to back him up. A man never knew. He would keep his eyes open.

"Get some light here, George," Mead said.

"How, damn it?"

Mead pointed to a corner of the chapel. There was a kerosene lamp there.

"S'pose there ain't no kerosene in it?"

"An' s'pose there is? You got the brains of jackrabbit, George."

George ambled over and picked up the lamp. He shook it. A heavy gurgle sounded inside.

"It's got kerosene in it."

"Well, light the goddamn thing then!"

Choate produced a box of matches and handed them to Clay.

When the wick flared up, George discovered there was no place to hang it. No nail or peg was sticking out of the walls or from the massive oak *viga* which supported the weight of the roof.

Long ago, when Father Gregorio was away for a few days buying salt and matches in Tucson, someone had built a fire in the chapel by pulling away an altar rail. When Father Gregorio came back he sighed and kicked the ashes into a corner. In the ashes Choate found a rusty nail. He handed it to Hart, who pounded the nail into the *viga* with his gun butt, just over the head of the Virgin. Then he hung the lamp from the nail with a pleased grin.

"How's that, Harry?"

Mead grunted.

Choate said, "We all finished with this big project?"

"Spit it out," Mead growled.

"I think you better listen to me, Mead. I have an idea you'll like."

"Yeah? What?" Mead said skeptically.

"That woman is going to make me and you a lot of money, Mead."

Mead laughed. When he stopped Choate began talking.

11

Slocum always approached everything warily. If possible he preferred to make a wide swing around it first, observing all tracks, listening for strange sounds, allowing his senses to behave like blotting paper and soak up any impression that impinged on them. Unimportant impressions were discarded. Others were brought into sharper focus and scrutinized with an intensity that was almost savage.

This was how Apaches behaved when they were out on a war party. Slocum liked the way they did things. That was how they had survived a murderous physical environment; that was how they had managed to keep fighting against soldiers with guns while they themselves had only bows and arrows. And that was how they had forced the Spaniards to withdraw south to Mexico.

A man could learn a lot from Apaches. In later years their method of looking around was to be summed up in a military maxim: *Time spent in reconnaissance is never wasted*.

So Slocum dismounted below the ridge overlooking Nuestra Señora de los Rios. He tied his horse to a piñon branch. He had circled so that the sun would be at his back and not reflect off anything so ordinary as a belt buckle. A piece of metal where none ought to be was a death warrant if some sharp-eyed sentry happened to be glancing in his direction.

He took off his sombrero and placed it beside the horse. He had already selected a manzanita growing at the crest. He slid behind the tree. Now the outline of his head would blend with the tangled branches of the manzanita.

He surveyed the mission inch by inch. He did not like the horses that had been hobbled and set to graze in the meadow, nor the fact that one set of tracks had joined the three tracks which had appeared after he had left for Fort Douglas. Four strange horses and a woman inside the chapel—it smelled bad.

There was no sign of Pilar.

Slocum did not like anything about the situation down there. He slid down the slope and sat cross-legged, like an Indian, while he did some more hard thinking. The last few miles he had traveled he had cut into the tracks of a horseman heading for the mission. And the left front shoe had a V-nick.

But who was he meeting?

The best thing to do would be to wait for nightfall and then become an Apache. Boots made an awful racket. Slocum reached for his saddlebag and took out the Apache moccasins he had cached there earlier. The moon would not rise till eleven. At nine, when it was fully dark, Slocum moved toward the mission in absolute silence. Anyone who had experience in Indian country would post a sentry. But anyone who knew Apaches knew they never made night attacks. Dawn raids were their specialty. This meant that, if anyone down in the mission were knowledgeable, there would be only one sentry at night. At sunrise, everyone would be awake.

Sure enough, as Slocum slithered into the vegetable garden and made his way along the rows of tomatoes and green peppers a few inches at a time, with his face pressed against the soil Father Gregorio had cultivated until only two weeks before, he suddenly saw the dark outline of a man sitting on the ground. The man had one leg drawn up; the other was stretched out in front. A carbine was set on the ground with the butt against the crotch. The barrel slanted across his left shoulder.

Slocum slid along the row of staked tomatoes. He turned his head slowly—in stalking, all movements had to be slow—and saw a profile. He felt disappointed that it was not Choate. He had a game to play out with Choate.

After an hour, someone appeared at the door. There was a kerosene lamp hanging in the chapel. The newcomer was framed against the yellow light.

The man on sentry duty said, "Aw, y' oughta know better'n that. Stand'n with light behint you! Any 'Pache out there, he'd stick an arrer in yore guts lickety-split."

The man inside the room said, "I ain't no tenderfoot. Ain't no 'Pache out there. Harry wants you to git a bucket an' some water from the river."

"Let 'im git his own goddamn water, he ain't crippled."

"He wants to dump it on that 'Pache gal. He figgers she'll come to faster. That cut she gave 'im—it's hurtin'. He's like a bear with a splinter in its paw. I'll go sentry."

"Aw, shit," said the other man. He ambled off into the darkness.

During the War Slocum had been slashed with a saber on his head at the Battle of the Wilderness. From time to time, he would lose control and go into a rage which, like a tidal wave hitting the coast, swept everything before it. He felt it coming now. In an effort to stop it he dug his fingernails into the soil and squeezed as hard as he could. His back muscles quivered with the strain as he sought to maintain control. To lose it now would be disastrous. When he relaxed his grip he was soaked with sweat.

Easy now, he told himself. *She's in there. She's probably unconscious. If I go in shooting she might get hurt. Best to go in invited.*

He worked his way backward. The man who had gone for water came back with the full bucket. The two entered the chapel together.

Slocum got to his feet and padded silently across the garden and over the wall surrounding the mission. He ran up the ridge, kicked off the moccasins, pulled on his boots, mounted, and came down the ridge and across the meadow at a fast trot. He made no effort to conceal his approach.

"Hello!" he called out loudly and cheerfully. "Anyone here?"

He heard the metallic clicks as the two men levered cartridges into their carbines.

"Hombres!" he shouted, *"hay comida?"*

Someone in the doorway of the chapel called out harshly, "Talk English!"

"Evenin', friend," Slocum said with a smile. "I asked if I could get a bite here."

"Come closer," a strange voice said. "Put both hands on yore horn an' keep 'em there."

So this was the man in charge, the one who had knocked Pilar unconscious.

Slocum obeyed. "No call for that, friend," he said, with the right injured air.

Mead paid no attention. "Sam."

"Yeah, Harry."

"Bring out the lamp."

Mead waited in silence. When Sam held the lamp up Mead carefully scrutinized Slocum.

"What you doin' ridin' at night?"

"Broke, lookin' for work. If it's all the same to you, gents, I guess I'll just keep movin'."

"I ast you a question, mister."

"Since there's only one of me, an' three of you, an' two coverin' me now, I'll answer it. Night's the best time to travel in Apache country." He talked louder than usual for two reasons: he wanted Pilar to know he was there, and he also wanted Choate to know. A man like Choate, suddenly surprised by a man whose horse he had killed, might start shooting.

But if Choate had advance notice, he might reconsider any impulsive action. A man accustomed to working with a couple of confederates hated to work alone, Slocum knew. A man like Choate would feel vulnerable, unable to relax around Mead and the other two.

Slocum's bet paid off.

"Evenin', John," Choate said. He stood in the doorway beside Mead, his hand on his gun butt.

"Evenin'," Slocum said. He pretended to be startled.

"Sorry I had to do that little thing," Choate said. "I had too much to drink. And things were going sour on me. I apologize."

"Oh, the hell with it," Slocum said. "You owe me two hundred and fifty for the horse and we'll call it quits."

"You'll get it, and double, for the trouble I caused you. Shake on it?" Choate was full of jubilant relief.

"Sure," Slocum said.

"I was sure you wouldn't get a horse. How the hell did you manage it?"

Slocum told him how he had sawed a section out of the adobe wall. He added, "Those two men of yours—"

"What about 'em?"

"They decided to take off for Tombstone."

"Yeah, they would. So you put the wall *back?*"

"Yep."

"By damn!" Mead exclaimed in admiration.

"This is John Slocum," Choate said.

"Slocum?" Mead said thoughtfully. "I do believe I've heard tell of a John Slocum. Ain't you the feller rustled a thousand head of prime beeves from Goodnight an' took 'em clear to Wyomin'?"

"Yeah."

"Well, now, anyone who c'n do that to that hard son of a bitch is someone I rightly admire. Pleased to meet you, John." He waved his wounded hand at his two men and they lowered their carbines. Mead was thinking that a man like Slocum would be a welcome addition. Mead was turning over in his mind a big operation: to join the rebel general Francisco Pereda. Pereda had approached him and said if Mead could produce a few good men with military experience to train his recruits, he would reward Mead with the ranch of Don Fernando Guzman, who ran over eighty thousand cattle on a million-acre ranch.

Mead knew that General Pereda had already seized the Guzman ranch. It seemed to Mead good sense to accept Pereda's offer, move into the Guzman hacienda, start training the recruits, then trail the cattle into Texas and sell them off five hundred cows at a time. It was a natural.

But for this he needed a skilled cowman. And he knew that Slocum qualified.

"You hungry?" Choate asked.

"Damn right."

"'Scuse my bad manners," Mead said. "Sam, get Slocum

some of that chicken and tomatoes. Put yore horse in the corral. We'll have some hot coffee ready soon's you come back."

They watched Slocum unsaddle his horse.

"Good man," Mead said.

"Yes," Choate said. Each man was planning on recruiting Slocum for himself. When Slocum came back he saw the carbines standing in a corner. The men had dropped their gunbelts and were stretched out on the stone floor. Slocum sat down close to the carbines. Mead handed him a chicken leg, a tomato, and a cup of hot black coffee. Slocum nodded his thanks and began to eat.

"Who's the woman?" he asked casually, jerking his head at Pilar. He had noticed that one black eye had opened and she was staring at him.

"Anybody's," Choate said, and burst into laughter.

Slocum rubbed his chin and let his fingertips slide vertically across his lips for a second, in the universal sign that meant silence. The black eye opened and closed in a wink. She had understood.

"Yeah," Mead said. "But only when I get finished."

"If she's smart she won't move a muscle when the war starts," Slocum said.

Harry tittered at the joke. Like the others, he was completely unaware of the double meaning. Slocum glanced at Pilar. She winked again. She understood that she was not to move.

"But first, she and I are going to talk a little," Choate said.

"You have persuasive powers?" Slocum asked gently.

The son of a bitch had tortured Father Gregorio. Now he was going to torture Pilar.

"Sometimes they die too soon," Choate said regretfully.

"It takes skill?"

"Yes, I think so. Especially with an Apache."

"You looking forward to it?"

"Yes. A real test of skill, believe me. We figure—" He looked at Mead, who nodded his head in permission. "We figure the old priest here told her where he cached something nice. We can't offer you much, because we made the deal before you showed up, but maybe we can use you. I'll give you something from my share, enough to take care of your horse and plenty more as well. And then we'll have a talk."

"Hold on a bit, Choate," Mead said harshly. "I got a deal for Slocum myself."

"Well," Slocum said, with hidden satisfaction, "I got a deal of my own comin' up." He stood up and tossed away his chicken bone.

He wiped his hands on his trouser legs. Now was not the time for a greasy hand to slide off a gun butt.

"What's that?" asked Choate with interest. He leaned forward.

"Wait till I get my *reata*," Slocum said. He was beginning to enjoy this. He went out and took the first *reata* he found, from Choate's saddle. He untied the rawhide thong holding it to the saddle skirt. He walked back inside. He took out his jackknife and cut off eight pieces of equal length—one set for each man. Pilar's eyes were open. She was watching intently, as were the four men.

"*Lista?* Ready?" he asked. She nodded imperceptibly.

"'Lista'?" Mead asked. "What's 'lista'?"

Slocum dropped the *reata* lengths in front of himself. He closed the jackknife and, holding it in his left palm, pulled his Colt.

"Here's the deal," he said. "First, everybody grab sky."

No one moved. He put a bullet so close to Mead's left ear that it seared the skin.

"Do it," Slocum said gently.

They slowly raised their hands.

"Mr. Mead."

Mead stared at Slocum with hatred.

"Mr. Mead, will you be good enough to step this way?"

Mead did not move.

"Mr. Mead, if you don't get your ass here in three seconds, I will put a bullet into your left knee."

Sometimes, when Slocum was afraid he would lose control, he spoke softly, as if the soothing tone could lull his violence. Mead recognized this quality immediately. He sat up and walked to Slocum.

"Now, Mr. Mead, listen good. I'm handing you this knife. You will cut the rawhide from the lady's wrists and ankles. When you finish you will close the knife and slide it across the floor to me. You will not try to harm the lady; you will not make any sudden moves. If you move faster than I like I will put a bullet in each knee. Then I will put a bullet into the foreheads of the other three gentlemen. Anyone doubt it?"

The three men shook their heads.

"All right," Slocum said. "Go."

Mead did all he was asked. When he was seated on the floor once more, Slocum asked Pilar if she could move her arms and legs.

"Sí."

"All right. I want the first volunteer. You will do, Mr. Choate. Slide across to the middle of the floor, lie on your belly, and put your hands on your back."

"What's up, Slocum?" For the first time Choate betrayed nervousness.

"I really don't know, Choate. Isn't that up to the lady? You're the one who tortured her foster father."

"Jesus, Slocum, you're not going to let *her* at me? She's a goddamn Apache!"

"Shut up." He nodded at Pilar. He had taught her a few simple knots on the ride north. She tied Choate efficiently.

"Mead. You volunteering?"

Mead didn't move. He was a brave man. The bullet hit the stone floor just in front of the man's testicles and fragmented. Particles of hot lead sprayed through his trouser legs. Pilar winced.

"The next one will blow 'em away," Slocum said. "How about a little friendly cooperation?"

Mead moved to the center of the floor. Pilar tied him up neatly. The other two men gave no trouble. Mead's face was pressed to the floor.

"You'll pay for this," he muttered.

"How?" Slocum asked, with only polite curiosity. "You're all going to die, and we're taking your horses. So how?"

"Jesus!" Hart said. Pilar took Slocum by the elbow and pulled him to a corner of the chapel. Above and to their right hung the kerosene lamp. Pilar's hair was matted with sweat and blood. Rage spilled over him when he saw that.

"What are you going to do?" she asked.

"Kill them."

"You must not!"

"The man named Choate tortured Father Gregorio. The man who hit you on the head is named Harry Mead. After he and the others finished raping you, they intended to kill you. He likes to kill women after raping them. I would be doing the world a favor."

"Do not say that. I am the one who has been injured, true?"

"True."

"I forgive them."

"Pilar—"

"And so I ask you to let them go," she said.

Words failed Slocum. Finally he said, "You realize what will happen? They will not rest till they find and kill me. Do you understand that?"

She stood with her hands clasped in front of her. Her great black eyes stared at him. He had never seen an Indian woman of such beauty. "Yes."

"And still you ask me?"

"Yes."

He stared at her. She said, "Father Gregorio must have forgiven them at the end. I know him. And so I forgive them. Let them go, John."

The thought of the treasure hidden somewhere nearby stayed his hand. If he were to kill the four men, she would never speak to him any more. No treasure. But if he let them go his life would go out like a snuffed candle if he ever turned his back on any one of them.

The idea of the treasure was more compelling.

"All right, they live, but on my terms."

The sky was lightening in the east. He went outside with her and saddled her Mormon horse. He put his saddle on Choate's horse, which was much better than his stolen cavalry mount. Next he opened the corral gate and slapped the four horses hard on their rumps. The cavalry horse whinnied and began trotting toward Fort Douglas. The other three horses paused for a moment, undecided, then followed the cavalry horse, which was already moving east at a fast clip. Choate and the others would never catch them.

Inside the chapel he gathered up all their guns. The men stared at him with hate-filled eyes, apprehensive. The kerosene lamp hanging over the Virgin had generated a stifling heat and they stank with sweat.

Choate had managed to wriggle close to Sam Hart. His wrists were near Hart's mouth. Slocum looked down and saw that the *reata* had been dampened by Hart's saliva. It would take Hart the better part of a day to chew through the strong leather. Then they'd have a sixty-mile walk across the desert to Tucson. It would be solid hell.

He looked them over one by one. No one said anything. Hart began to tremble. Slocum turned his hard gaze on Mead, who stared back without fear.

"*Adios,*" Slocum said abruptly.

"No, Slocum," Choate said, "it's *hasta la vista.*"

Slocum turned back and, as a farewell gesture, he pulled off their boots. He carried them outside, found a dense clump of manzanita a hundred years away, and hurled the boots into it. Nothing but kangaroo rats and chuckwallas would ever see them again. Now Choate and Mead would have something else to hate him for.

12

Slocum and Pilar sat just below the crest of the ridge overlooking the mission. He had washed the clotted blood from her hair in the river. Her headache had stopped; there was no concussion, then. When she bathed in the river he managed to refrain from staring at her naked brown body.

"What will they do now?" she asked him.

"They'll work loose by tonight. Then they'll head for Tucson. They need horses, guns, saddles, and boots. Don't forget boots." He grinned at the picture of four cursing men tiptoeing gingerly across the cactus flats and sharp stones.

"Won't it be dangerous to move back in?"

He looked at her with a puzzled expression.

"These men. They hate you," she went on.

Slocum smiled. "Yes," he said. "But there's no more chickens. And why would they think we'll stay? We buried the man who knew about the treasure. So they'll make a fresh start somewhere. First they'll start by robbing a bank or a stagecoach." He grinned. "And four dirty men without boots are not going to hold up a bank with clubs."

She had a lovely smile. Then she said, "These men— why do you think they'll leave tonight?"

"They can't carry enough water to travel in the heat. And the sun would make the sand so hot they couldn't walk on it. They can make twenty miles the first night."

"I don't want to go back there. I want to go back to Hermosillo."

His face hardened with a savagery that startled her. He bent down and gripped her shoulders. "Listen! *You* wanted the treasure of the Virgin. I spent a lot of time on this. I'm not going to walk away now. We're going to stay here till we find it." His green eyes burned. "I lost a good horse. *Claro?*"

The power of the man settled over her.

"Claro," she finally said. "But no more than a week. Agreed?"

He relaxed. "Agreed."

He looked over the ridge top. They were still inside the mission. "Poor Sam," he said. "He must have the most overworked pair of jaws in the world."

When her smile came it was brilliant. He had saved her life, saved her from rape, cleansed her wound, and fed her. He looked up and caught her looking at him.

She flushed. The man fascinated her. She began to look forward to the week she would spend alone with him in the mission.

But Pilar was still nervous thinking about the return of the four men, even though they had left during the night.

Slocum took care of that. In the storeroom he found several large balls of twine, left over from the days when Father Gregorio used to tie the tomato plants to their stakes. With the twine and the large collection of empty bottles Father Gregorio had saved for forty years Slocum built an alarm system.

He broke the stakes into sixteen-inch lengths. He sharpened them on one end and drove them deep into the ground under the top of the meadow grass so that they were invisible. He set them ten feet apart until the entire mission was surrounded. He tied the heavy twine from one stake to the next. Every ten feet he tied a group of three empty bottles. Suspended, they would crash against each other whenever a man's stealthy foot might stumble against the taut twine.

Pilar didn't think it would work. He told her to walk across the meadow toward the mission and listen. It came as a shock to her, even though she had been expecting it, when her ankle hit the twine and the bottles jangled and crashed. She looked at him. She was beginning to admire this man very much.

"Exactly what did Father Gregorio say about the treasure?" Slocum asked. "Tell me everything he said, no matter how trivial it might sound."

"All I remember is that he kept saying with a smile that *she* knows where it is. I thought nothing of it—of course she knows where it is. It was hers; why shouldn't she know?"

Slocum lit the lamp. It was still hanging on the *vega* from its nail right where the four men had left it. The night was chilly.

"I don't want to sleep here," Pilar said.

Slocum understood. "Out in the meadow?" he suggested.

"Under the peach tree."

He reached up to turn down the wick in the lamp, and out of the corner of his eye he noticed something which should not have been there.

"What's the matter?"

He held up his hand for silence. He was thinking hard.

And suddenly he knew. *Wax.* There was candle wax on the back of the Virgin's head. People burned candles in churches. There was always wax where the votive candles were burning. But why should there be any wax on the Virgin's head?

He unhooked the lamp and moved it closer to the wax. Thus he found the key to the treasure of the Virgin.

The heat of the lamp, placed close to the back of her carved wooden head, had melted the wax. The wax had closed up a hole which had been drilled into the back of the head.

Slocum held the lamp close to the hole. He saw the end of a tightly rolled cylinder of parchment.

"We found the treasure!" he said.

Pilar turned pale.

He hung the lamp on the nail and pried out the parchment with the tip of his jackknife.

He unhooked the lamp and set it on the stone floor. The parchment was unrolled and spread flat. It originally had been covered with a long Latin letter from the bishop in Chihuahua, requesting a list of data from an early priest. Father Gregorio had scraped the parchment clean. Then he had sketched the mission between its two rivers, the valley, the mountain, the huge rock formations to be used as sign-posts, and, finally, the old mine opening into which he had inserted the treasure. Underneath he had written, "Everything she owns is inside. It is all hers, for the glory of God."

"Por Dios," Pilar whispered.

Slocum thought of the final irony: If Choate had not tried to find the treasure, no one would have driven a nail into the *viga,* and thus hang the lamp just where its heat would melt the wax. And, final and most beautiful irony, the wax had melted when Choate was only a few feet away.

Pilar used the rest of the evening to carve Father Gregorio's name on the old board. Her head was tilted to one side to catch the sound of glass tinkling. Slocum pulled the blanket over his head and fell asleep immediately. She paused in her work and looked at the exhausted man. If she had not taken her vows, she thought—She pushed the thought away.

Several miles to the north, the four men limped slowly and painfully in their stocking feet in the darkness. They had stopped talking about what they would do to Slocum when they caught up with him. Cactus needles had penetrated their soft soles. Pebbles and stones had bruised them. In the dark, there was no way they could avoid jumping cholla. Three times big diamondbacks had coiled and rattled at their approach. The men made a wide detour, stepping onto more cactus. Slocum had mentioned to Pilar that, with any luck, a rattler ought to bite at least one of the men, but her face froze. She did not like this kind of talk.

Each man had picked up a stick.

Mead said, "If you didn't talk so much the goddamn rattlers wouldn't hear us comin'."

"Snakes don't have ears," Choate said. His feet were almost numb.

"You talk like you know all there is to know, Choate. I truly don't like it."

Choate stopped. The others halted. The moon had not yet risen. The Milky Way, which the Mexicans called the

Road of the Ghosts, curved overhead in a majestic, pulsing white arch. There was enough light to see dark masses of chaparral and the high dark bulk of the mountains. They were walking across a desolate flat in order to intersect the primitive and rarely traveled road which went north to Tucson.

"I'm hongry," Sam said.

"Goddamn idjit," Mead said, without passion.

Sam, usually calm, flared up. "An' I'm tired of bein' nagged at, Harry! I warn ya!"

Mead said coldly, "We're all havin' a hard time. Our feet hurt an' we're busted an' we ain't got no horses. Now shut up and keep on walkin'."

Sam subsided.

Mead said, "Where'd you say that road was, Choate?"

"It ought to be two, three miles from here, as I remember."

"I hope you're right. You're right 'bout so many things, Choate. Like the treasure back there. And tying up with Slocum. An' 'bout how snakes don't have no ears."

They began a painful crawl down a rocky slope, from which centuries of rain had washed away all the soil, leaving stones and dense stands of *chamisa,* beavertail cactus, and ocotillo. The trail twisted around each bush which barred its way. Diamondbacks, night hunters, stalked lizards and ground squirrels. Twice more during the night rattlers coiled and rattled. Mead hated rattlesnakes. He said, "I'd like five minutes alone with Slocum. I surely would."

"Wouldn't we all," Choate said.

Two hours later, luck arrived. They reached the Tucson road. Five minutes later they saw two horses outlined against the sky. They neared slowly. The horses were not riding mounts. Each horse was munching oats in a nose bag. Pulled off the road was a wagon. Someone was snoring in the back. They approached silently.

In the starlight Choate read, painted on the wagon side, S. JACOBSON SUNDRIES.

"It's a Jew peddler," Sam whispered.

"Two on each side," Mead said.

When they were in place, Mead said, "Now!"

Jacobson struggled to get free, but he could not. In the front near his pillow was a double-barreled shotgun and a kerosene lantern. A box of matches lay beside it.

"Light it," Mead said.

The wide, terrified eyes of the peddler stared at them. The wagon was full of wooden boxes filled with thread, scissors, bolts of fabric, needles, women's hats, pots and pans—everything a lonely ranch woman might like.

"We ain't gonna hurt you, mister," Mead said soothingly. "We want your money an' your wagon, is all."

Jacobson reached inside his coat pocket and handed over his worn leather wallet. Mead counted three hundred and twelve dollars. "Good, good," he said. With the sale of the contents of the wagon, the wagon and the horses to people who would ask no questions he estimated he would clear over a thousand dollars, enough to equip his men.

"Any more money?" he asked.

"You got it all," Jacobson muttered.

"Pretty dangerous, sleepin' alone in this here country," Mead said in a friendly manner.

Jacobson shrugged. "I go where business is good."

"Yeah, I s'pose. Got 'ny boots?"

"No. Just for womenfolks."

"I'm sorry to hear that." Mead reached down and pulled Jacobson to his feet.

"Over the side," he said crisply. "We gonna leave you here."

"Here, in the *desert?*"

"Walk at night like we do. Step that way a bit," Mead said, and shot Jacobson in the back with both barrels of the shutgun. He told Sam and George to hitch up the horses.

"We gotta make time," he said. "The sooner we get to Tucson, the sooner we'll be back. And when we do, I'm gonna show you how Quantrill could stretch out a bit of ticklin'. Just hang around, Choate 'n' watch. Move, you goddamn horses!"

13

Venus was lit up with a buttery glow by the still invisible sun. Slocum dropped a loop on his horse. It crawfished twice around the corral out of sheer exuberance before it settled down. Slocum slid down and lashed a pick to the skirt.

Slocum filled their canteens in the river. The water was clear and cold. Next, he set their course for the V-shaped notch in the range to their east. That was Father Gregorio's first directive. As they rode toward it the sun rose and fit into the notch like a front bead on a rifle.

They rode to the notch. When they got there he pulled the map from his saddlebag and unrolled it. Once at the notch, they had to look to the right. There would be two large boulders. Once lined up, sight along their tops. A rock ledge would be seen. Go to the ledge. Slocum had the directions memorized.

Their horses leaned into the slope. The powerful muscles between Pilar's thighs bunched and relaxed. It excited her. The sudden perception made her flush. She was feeling less and less like a nun. Perhaps it was a mistake for her to have come with this John Slocum. But then, given the chance to bring back the treasure of the Virgin to Hermosillo, who could resist? If it was God's will that she be with this man, she would accept it.

"Here's the ledge," Slocum said. "Then it says, 'Look to your left at the south end of the ledge. One hundred feet away are three piñons. Just below them are three large stones arranged in a triangle. Break open a hole in the center of the pines. Inside is the treasure of the Virgin. Bless the man who shall return it to Mother Church. Father Gregorio.'"

They saw the three piñons. Slocum judged them to be around thirty years old. They dismounted. Slocum took the pick and swung it. It sank into the hard-baked soil beside the tree. In a few minutes the tree's roots had been severed. He put down the pick and took a good grip on the trunk. She watched his back and shoulder muscles knot and swell.

Suddenly the tree broke free. A cold blast of air flowed strongly from the twelve-inch gap.

"The mine opening," Slocum said.

Pilar crossed herself.

In five minutes Slocum had pried out the other two trees.

"I want to go in first," Pilar said.

Slocum nodded. He took a candle and a box of matches from his saddlebag. "Watch for snakes," he warned. She paid no attention in her excitement.

She went in. The candle flame fluttered in the draft. Slocum followed. "Watch the floor," he said. "Sometimes there's a vertical shaft."

She recoiled and backed into him. At the feel of her body he could not help feeling aroused. Startled, she hesitated a moment before moving ahead once more. She felt as if her face were on fire.

She moved ahead, followed closely by Slocum, who gripped her belt. She understood that he was worried about her possible fall into a shaft. She leaned back imperceptibly into his grip.

The mine curved to the left. She halted abruptly and gasped. She lifted the candle high. The warm yellow glow was reflected in myriad tiny darts of brilliance from the pile of massive gold candlesticks and from the facets of diamonds. Even the big rose pearls on the Virgin's dress picked up the candle's yellow gleam.

"*Dios mio!*" cried Pilar, sinking to her knees.

Sixty-five miles to the northeast Harry Mead lay on the bed of the best room of the Territorial Hotel, the best hotel in Tucson. Choate sat nearby in the ornate red plush armchair. His legs were outstretched and he was blowing smoke rings. Both George Clay and Sam Hart were sitting in straight-backed side chairs. None of the men were wearing their new boots. All had bandages on their feet. The boots were still too tight when pulled on over the bandages.

"What'll we do now?" Hart asked. "Now we got horses an' guns?"

"Use 'em," Mead said.

George Clay let out a short bark of laughter.

"How?" Choate asked.

"Hell, that's easy. Kill Slocum."

"How?" Choate asked again. When no one responded he blew some smoke rings. "Not so easy, is it?" he said. "Even with four of us."

"Aw, shit," Mead said. "I never saw no one I couldn't kill easy if I wanted to."

"Especially a big, dangerous peddler," Choate said.

Mead turned on his side and stared at Choate. "I *like* to kill Yankees," he said. "I did it all through the dang war. An' I don't have to stop 'cause of Appomattox, neither, Choate."

"Mr. Mead," Choate said, "let us think real hard about Slocum. We have scores to settle. I want to settle them and then go about my business. I want to thank you for my new outfit, by the way."

Mead waved a languid hand.

"But I don't see *any* plans for Slocum," Choate finished.

"It's our feet! Trouble is, we're all right in the saddle, but afoot ain't much we c'n do. We can't do no runnin'. Can't hardly walk. We jus' gotta wait till they heal, is all damn it."

"How long?"

"I figger three, four days. We got 'enough money left fer that. So take it easy, Choate. Don't keep on naggin' or I'll get my dander up. You hear?"

Choate lit another cigar.

"An' don't dump them cigar ashes on the floor!" Mead shouted, white with fury. "This ain't no pigsty! It's a high-class hotel. Jesus Christ, Choate how was you brought up, anyways?"

Hart stood up, picked up a water glass from the oak bureau, and set it down on the flat arm of Choate's chair.

"Let's have a little quiet, Harry," he said, and sat down.

Mead suddenly chuckled. "Sam, Sam," he said, "sometimes I think you got more sense than me an' Choate put together."

Slocum counted ten huge candlesticks. Each one had been designed to hold a candle six inches across at the base. He lifted one candlestick. He judged its weight at least forty pounds. He ran a thumbnail across it. Solid gold. He set it down. The robe, with its heavy encrustation of diamonds, rubies, emeralds, and gold thread, weighed another forty pounds or so. With those items he could buy himself the biggest ranch in Texas if he wished. He could buy half of Costa Rica!

"John," she said finally, "it is too big for the convent. It will have to go to the catherdral in Mexico City."

Slocum promised himself that the cathedral would never see it. He went out to get some food from the saddlebag.

It would be best to wait till nightfall before bringing the treasure down the mountain. Someone might see it and wonder what all those bright shiny flashes were. They could wait. He had taken the last of the chickens and the tomatoes for food.

While she ate she gave him a look of such warm affection and trust that he felt uncomfortable. His only intent in going along with her had been to clear off with the treasure if they found it.

"You are very quiet, John."

"Thinking, Pilar."

Unlike most women, she did not ask what he was thinking about. If he chose to tell her, that would be his business, not hers.

"When is sunset?"

"Six hours."

"And moonrise?"

"Two hours later."

"I want to stay here until the moon rises," she said.

Slocum thought, Here's an Apache who likes the night.

"When I lived here Father Gregorio told me that the moon was the eye of God watching me. I want to see it once more." She paused and folded her arms under her breasts.

"Because I will never come back to Nuestra Señora de los Rios again." Her eyes grew shiny with tears. "I can never do anything like this again. Even once is a great sin."

She fell silent. She clearly wanted to be alone.

"I better look at the horses," he said. Once outside he sat down against a rock and tried to decide what to do. Take it all? Take some? Escort her back? If so, all the way? To Magdalena? And where would he sell the gold? Tucson? San Francisco? There were arguments for and against each place. Then, what about the jewels? Slocum knew very little about gem values. Should he go to New York? Europe?

His mind buzzed. The sun had gone down and the warmth had leaked out of the mountain air. He stood up. The granite ledge still held the sun's warmth, and would continue to hold it for hours.

Inside the mine, she was asleep. She had opened the top three buttons of her shirt for coolness. He stood above her and looked down at her half-exposed breasts. They were a pale copper color with dark red nipples perched on each apex. He felt a hot sensation begin in his groin.

She woke suddenly.

"Moon's rising," he said thickly. She buttoned her shirt, avoiding looking at the bulge in his pants. He carried out the candlesticks and the robe and lashed them securely to the saddles. When he went in again to tell her all was ready his passage alarmed a big diamondback which had crawled out of a horizontal fissure in the rock ledge. The snake had slid down to drink from a small pool fifty feet away. Slocum's movement disturbed the snake. It slithered out onto the ledge and then went into a massive brown coil behind one of the rocks pried out by Slocum.

Pilar stood up and walked to the entrance. Slocum stayed behind and blew out the candle as she crawled through the opening.

As she rested on her left knee, preparing to stand, the big diamondback struck. The long, curved fangs went deep into her left thigh and the huge venom sacs contracted. The impact was like being struck by a fist. At first she thought Slocum had struck her for some reason she did not understand. When she turned to look at him she realized that he was too far away. Then she saw the rattler flowing back into its dark crevice.

She screamed and pointed to her thigh. Slocum bent down and saw two small drops of yellow venom on her pants. He did not waste time looking for the diamondback. He pulled her back into the mine. He needed light and he didn't want anyone noticing a candle flame on the side of an uninhabited mountain. He lit the candle.

This was no time for false modesty. He unbuckled her belt and pulled off her pants. On the inside of her left thigh he saw the two fang marks. He opened his jackknife, lay flat between her outspread legs, and, without any warning, made two quick cross incisions at each fang mark. Then he started to suck the poison as hard as he could. He spat out venom and blood. He squeezed her thigh to force as much venom as he could to the surface, then sucked again and again till his lips were exhausted. The pain had not yet started.

Suddenly he was aware that she was sexually excited.

He did not know how long he could keep himself from screwing her. He had better put her back into her convent at Hermosillo before she lost her virginity. For that he did not want to be responsible.

He stood up and pulled her pants up. She stared up at him, opened her mouth to say something, and suddenly let out a groan of pain.

So the poison was still there. There would be serious complications if the diamondback bite ran its usual course.

He had better get her into a comfortable place. He helped her from the mine. By the time he had put her into her saddle the pain had climbed to her hips and was rising. The leg was beginning to swell. She was sweating and biting her lips to keep from screaming.

He took her to the chapel and put her on a blanket. He filled the canteen with fresh water and put it beside her. It looked as if the leg would get worse; that was the way these bites ran. They would have to stay there until she got better. *If* she got better. Tomorrow he would have to get good food to give her strength for her fight against the poison. He would make a nourishing soup from quail. There were no more chickens left; Choate and Meads' party had killed them all.

14

Mead pulled on his boots and swore. His feet still hurt, but not as bad as they had yesterday.

He tried to stand up. *"Jesus!"* he said, and sat down again and pulled off the boots.

Choate sat in the armchair looking at the ceiling. Sam Hart and Geroge Clay were snoring on the floor. Someone knocked.

"Come in," Mead growled. A man entered who wore the shoulder-length hair of an Apache and the blue jeans and checkered shirt of a white cowpuncher. His eyes were a cold gray. He was five feet ten inches tall and had the wide shoulders of an Apache. He wore a Navajo necklace of turquoise and squash blossoms. On his left wrist he wore a bow guard. Mead wasn't sure whether the man was heavily tanned, or whether he was a half-breed. The man wore an old gunbelt and a well oiled Colt.

"You Choate?" he asked.

Mead jerked his thumb.

"Hello, Joe Charley!"

Joe Charley was a Mexican who had been captured by White Mountain Apaches when he was six years old. He had grown up with them, become a warrior, and left abruptly after a savage quarrel with a Chiricahua war chief named Tedashke. Next he volunteered his services to the cavalry as a scout. He was one of the best trackers in the southwest. Choate had sent word to Fort Grant that if Joe Charley were available he had some well-paying work for him.

Joe Charley stood and waited. He had patience. Choate liked that. It was one of the essential qualities of a good tracker.

"Joe Charley is a tracker," Choate told Mead. "The best."

"Why do we need a tracker?" Mead asked.

"How are you at following someone's trail afoot these days?"

Mead grunted.

"And besides tracking," Choate went on, "he's got no objection to finishing up the job, if need be."

"'If need be,'" Joe Charley repeated with a wide grin.

"How much you askin'?" Mead said.

"What's wrong with everyone's feet?" Joe Charley abruptly asked. "I smell linimint 'n' iodine."

"We all took a little walk," Mead said. "We don't take it kindly."

"Someone took *all* your boots?" the tracker asked.

"Yeah."

"An' horses?"

"Yeah."

"*One* man?"

There was an embarrassed silence.

"My oh my," Joe Charley said.

"I ast you how much," Mead said, with an edge to his voice.

"This man, he's pretty good?"

"Lucky—just lucky," Mead said.

Choate looked wearily at Mead. Then he said, "Yeah, Joe Charley. He's plenty good."

"You want me to find 'im?"

"Joe Charley," Choate said, "we got to move fast. Our feet are pretty bad. We need someone who can track, fight on his feet, and so forth. We'll all go together."

"You want a guardian?"

Mead opened his mouth to retort.

Choate said, "Joe Charley, we'll pay double what you get as a scout."

"How many days you figger?"

"Seven, eight."

Joe Charley had a white girlfriend named Rose. She worked as a whore in the back of a saloon in Benson. If he gave her a nice ring she had her eye on she would only screw him, she had told Joe Charley last week.

"When we leavin'?" he asked.

"Soon's you're ready."

"I'm ready now, mister."

"Well, then," Choate said, turning to Mead.

Pilar's left thigh had almost doubled in size. It was a dull red. The pain was excruciating. The weight of the blanket was agonizing. She lay on the blanket with her leg bare.

Slocum had gone out and shot two quail on the far side of the meadow. Even though he knew where the glass tripline was, he almost stumbled against the twine. The quail meat was juicy since the birds had been eating well on grass seed and berries. He made a rich soup out of it and fed it to her with a spoon.

The pain intensified as the hours passed. They would have to stay there until she could travel. Slocum found a safe place to hide the treasure. It was simple. He just dug a new grave. In it he set the robe in a burlap sack, together with the candlesticks. He filled it in and made a simple cross out of two narrow boards.

When he came back with the shovel he noticed two wooden boxes in a corner of the storeroom. The words CAUTION DYNAMITE had been crudely lettered on their sides. His first thought was that Father Gregorio, judging from the wild profusion of odds and ends in the storeroom, was an ecclesiastical packrat. Somewhere, probably in an abandoned mine office, he had found two perfectly good, empty wooden boxes which had once held dynamite.

One of the top boards had been pried loose and casually nailed back again. Slocum picked up a claw hammer and pried up the same board.

Inside were neat rows of dynamite. Slocum looked at them thoughtfully.

Very slowly, very carefully, he pulled out one stick. He turned it over and felt it with the tip of a finger. *Crystals.* He put it back again with the greatest of care. When he finished he was sweating with tension.

Dynamite is that most unstable of explosives—nitroglycerin—mixed with a kind of clay called kieselguhr. Pure nitroglycerin will explode if dropped. It is so unstable and so sensitive to any shock that people used to say it would explode if a man gave it a dirty look.

Mixed with kieselguhr it becomes very stable. It can be dropped, smashed with a hammer, or thrown into a fire. It will not explode. For that it needs a blasting cap and a fuse.

When dynamite is stored in boxes the nitroglycerin slowly settles downwards with the force of gravity. When it arrives at the bottom it then crystallizes. The crystals are pure nitroglycerin. A blow with a hammer will set it off. Or, if someone wants to cut a stick in half, the mere pressure of the knife blade will explode it.

Good mine management makes sure that each box is turned upside down once a month. This ensures the equal distribution of nitroglycerin in each stick.

Slocum stared at the two deadly boxes. Father Gregorio had found them, ripped one open to see what it contained— he probably did not know the English word "dynamite"— and then pounded the loose board in again. He did not realize, of course, how close he and the mine office had been to being immediately pulverized. He must have packed the boxes on his mule, then slid and jerked them over a mile or more of rough trail. Then he probably dropped them casually on the stone floor. He never knew how close he and the chapel came to disappearing in one huge explosion. Slocum put the boxes very carefully into a corner where he would be sure never to stumble over them accidentally.

Shifting the boxes revealed a rectangular pattern in the storeroom floor. A two-foot square was traced in the stone. At one end of the rectangle a hole the size of a forefinger had been drilled. Slocum bent down and pulled. The stone pivoted up and a wave of cool air spilled upward. Slocum lit a candle and lowered himself into the hole. A tunnel four feet tall extended in the darkness toward the river.

He followed it. Oak beams formed the uprights every three feet. They supported horizontal members. After a hundred feet the tunnel made a sharp bend to the right. A square of light appeared. He was at the edge of the river-bank. The opening was well camouflaged by a dense stand of reeds. Resting on two small sawhorses near the exit was a small boat. Two oars lay beside the boat. The dry air had kept the boat from rotting. The hull needed a couple of days in the water in order to swell and stop the leaks. But even if he put it directly into the water and used it, the leaks could easily be bailed out.

Slocum set the candle down and sat back on his heels. No doubt, when the mission had been built, the good fathers had realized they were in hostile country. They could be martyrs, but a way out if necessary could also find favor in the eyes of God. Probably it had never been used. Why else was the boat there?

Maybe by the time Father Gregorio had come the secret had been forgotten. Slocum turned and went back along the tunnel. When he closed the trap door he pushed dust into the cracks and shoved a few Papago grain baskets over the trap door. No one would ever find the door unless they knew it was there. Satisfied, Slocum went to check on Pilar.

Her leg had turned black and had swollen even more. Slocum felt terror. She was gasping, tossing her head restlessly from one side to the other, and moaning in pain. He knelt beside her. She seized his hand.

"I thought you had left me!"

"Never, Pilar."

Once, when he was living with some Apaches, he had accompanied Ukashe, a medicine man, to search for plants and herbs for healing and for ceremonies. The inner bark of an obscure brown herb growing along arroyos, Ukashe said, was good for pain and for snakebite. One boiled it with water, made it into a poultice, and placed it on the bad flesh.

But the herb grew only at high altitudes. There was a peak twenty miles away. It looked as if it went up ten or eleven thousand feet. He hated to leave her alone, but he had no choice. If he left now, with luck he would be back tomorrow night. He filled two buckets with water from the river and put them beside her. He placed a pot with some quail broth there too.

"Where are you going?"

"For medicine."

"Hurry back."

For protection he gave her the shotgun. He felt her face. It was hot with fever.

By seven next morning he was halfway up the mountain. The going became worse. By nine he tied his horse to a cottonwood so it could munch the leaves. By ten-thirty he had spotted the brown herb in a dried-up arroyo bed.

15

Thirty miles to the northeast, Mead reined in and held up his hand.

The others stopped. Three packhorses carrying plenty of food, blankets, and tarpaulins followed. Joe Charley had told Mead he wanted to move in comfort.

They had left Tucson at sunrise. Mead had been in a fever of anxiety to get hold of Slocum; he had not even permitted a breakfast stop.

"We eat right now," Joe Charley said, "or I head right back faster'n a bear goin' to shit in the woods."

"That's why I'm stoppin'," Mead said. He had sensed the men's growing anger, so he had yielded before it could become too late.

Sam Hart was the outfit's cook. In ten minutes he had bacon frying, beans heating, and coffee coming to a boil. He even had some dried-apple pie.

"Good feedin'," Joe Charley said. He scraped up a spoonful of beans. The others were sweating in the increasing heat of the sun. Joe Charley did not sweat. He was in perfect physical condition and had burned every spare ounce of fat off his lean, hard, muscular body.

They could see Slocum's mountain to the southwest. They did not know he was up there at that moment, cramming herbs into his saddlebag.

Mead gulped down his food like a famished dog. Choate ate slowly, chewing carefully. Mead waited restlessly. "You eat like a schoolmarm, Choate," he sneered, making mincing motions with his mouth. Then he added in a falsetto, "Chew real nice, boys 'n' girls!"

"We better find Slocum soon," Choate said mildly, "because it looks like you got hydrophobia and should be put out of your misery."

No one laughed. Mead was too dangerous when he got into one of his moods. It was not yet noon, but the temperature had climbed to a hundred and twenty-eight.

Joe Charley had never been to the Papago country before. He swiveled his head back and forth, memorizing. One of the qualities of a good tracker was an absolute mastery of the terrain. That way a man could decide where the quarry might go to ground and be there to greet him.

He saw a cactus desert tilting to the southwest. Ocotillo, beavertail, and saguaro were scattered everywhere. At the far edge was a range of peaks thrusting up like a long knife blade with pieces snapped off in an erractic fashion.

Slocum was riding down one of the peaks as the four men were finishing their meal. As soon as he reached level ground he put his horse at a fast trot.

• • •

Pilar woke. It was late afternoon. She was constantly thirsty. Her leg had swollen even more and the skin had cracked open because of the mounting pressure from the poisoned flesh underneath. She fell asleep and woke up again a few minutes later.

For a few moments she did not know why she was awake. Then she realized she had heard the glass bottles clanging. Someone had breached the warning line. She picked up the shotgun and cradled it under her left elbow. Slowly she pulled herself along the floor, dragging her useless leg. When she reached the chapel window she pulled herself erect. Holding on to the window ledge for support, she looked. A man was walking slowly toward the chapel with a Colt in his hand. A hundred feet in back of him, four men sat their horses and waited. One of them was Harry Mead. Her heart began to beat wildly.

She remembered what Slocum had told her. "It takes a lot of skill to handle a Colt or carbine. Lots of men miss. But no one misses with a shotgun. The pellets make a big spread and tear a hole the size of a cantaloupe. *Everyone* is afraid of a shotgun."

"I will not kill anyone," Pilar had said.

"You don't have to. Point it up in the air and pull the trigger. If they have any sense, they'll just go away."

She rested the barrel of the shotgun on the bottom sill of the window, aimed the barrel above the strange man's head, and pressed the trigger.

Slocum's horse was lathered with sweat. He had pushed the pace to a canter. When he reached the crest of the ridge overlooking the mission he stopped, dismounted, took off his sombrero and crawled up to the ridge top for a quick look. At that moment Pilar fired the shotgun.

Slocum saw four men sitting their horses at the far edge of the meadow. Another man had been walking toward the mission. The man put his hand to his face, turned suddenly, and walked quickly back to join the others. Just as he turned, the air brought the sound of the shotgun blast to Slocum.

Good, he thought. *The bottle alarm must have worked. Whoever they are, they won't rush the mission in daylight. Not with a shotgun in there. They'll wait for a night attack.*

In the ordinary course of his business Slocum would also have waited for darkness. Then he would have attacked them from the rear and taken them one by one. A knife attack would be best. He could kill each one without alerting the others. But with Pilar needing the medicine so desperately, he'd have to go in right now.

At least he had the secret tunnel. Slocum backed down the slope.

When Pilar fired high into the air she did not know that the shotgun pellets would travel in an arc. Several pellets struck Joe Charley's face. At that distance the impact was so slight it was as if someone had tossed a handful of gravel at him.

But to Joe Charley, told that Slocum was there, it meant that Slocum had deliberately fired as a warning. Joe Charley moved back. He was convinced that Slocum had figured out the arc that the pellets would follow in their flight.

When he reached Mead he was feeling his face to see if the skin had been broken.

"He get you?" Mead asked.

Joe Charley shook his head.

"Damn good shootin'," he said. "He's got some kinda tripwire out there, looks like. Heard somethin' make a noise."

"Well," Mead said, "we'll just have to wait for dark. Come at 'em from all sides at once." He looked at Choate challengingly.

Choate nodded agreement.

"All right," Mead said. "Let's fall back, case he brings out a rifle. An' keep a sharp lookout all the time."

The force of the powerful recoil knocked Pilar backward. The pain in her leg was agonizing. She screamed. After a while she managed to get to her feet again, but she could not stand. Too weak to do anything but lie down, she crawled back to her blanket, dragging the black, misshapen leg. Finally on her back, she placed the shotgun by her side and wondered when Slocum would come back.

Slocum made a big circle behind the ridge. Finally, after an hour of hard riding, he debouched where an arroyo ran at right angles to the river. He tied the horse's reins to a manzanita. He took off the saddlebags which he had filled with the herbs.

Sudden cloudbursts high up in the mountains frequently uprooted trees and lodged them against the arroyo walls. Slocum found one just the right size for his purpose. He pulled it free. Then he stripped and rolled up his clothes, boots, and gun. He jammed everything into a wedge-shaped crotch, set the saddlebags across the trunk, and pulled it slowly into the river. He broke several branches from a nearby cottonwood and jammed them among the branches of his craft so that the profuse leaves would break up his outline.

Then he shoved off. The current flowed at a placid two miles an hour. An hour passed before he saw the mission in the distance. He kicked underwater. The powerful beat of his legs forced his tree trunk into the thick growth of reeds which masked the tunnel entrance.

He saw the men with their horses and pack animals two hundred yards down river. They were resting below the top of the bank and could not be seen from the mission. He recognized Mead and Choate as well as the two others. He did not know the fifth man. The four men he recognized had taken off their boots and socks and were soaking their feet in the water. Slocum permitted himself a brief smile. He wished he could have heard their comments as they hobbled their way barefoot across the desert, but a man could not experience all the pleasures of life.

The fifth man was sitting a few feet from the others. He had kept his boots on. He looked dark enough to be an Indian or a half-breed. Slocum judged that he had joined up in his capacity as a tracker. He would have liked to drift by with the camouflaged log for a better look, but that new man seemed too observant. Unlike the others, he constantly kept looking around, checked wind direction, and he stood up occasionally for a look all around at a greater height. He could be dangerous. The others just sat in a row.

The man, Slocum was sure, was like a hunting falcon. His job was to look for game and, if spotted, to bring it down. Falcons were rewarded with meat. In this case, Slocum thought the man had been promised a share of the treasure as an inducement. He did not know then that Joe Charley would have hunted him down for pure pleasure.

It was time to take care of Pilar. Slocum pulled aside the reeds and crawled into the tunnel. Then he remembered he had blocked the trap door. He could wait for nightfall to get into the mission, but that would mean a wait of seven hours. And every hour counted with snakebite.

When he reached the trap door he picked up a small stone and knocked up at the stone. *Bang, bang-bang.* John Slocum. *Bang bang-bang.* John Slocum.

She heard him. She did not think an enemy would announce his presence so openly to someone who had fired at him. If John Slocum had come back—and he should be back by now—he would have avoided the men in the meadow and found some other way to come in. She picked up the shotgun and crawled toward the storeroom, dragging her bad leg behind her.

The tapping went on. She located it and pushed aside the boxes that covered it. She tapped the stone with the shotgun stock in the same rhythm Slocum was using, then sat back to watch. But first she leveled the barrel at the floor.

The stone pivoted. Slocum's head appeared. Pilar burst into tears. He carried her back and prepared the poultice.

Early in the evening someone yelled "Hey! Slocum!" Mead had cut some birch bark and made an effective megaphone out of it.

Slocum looked up from Pilar. He had just placed the third poultice on her leg. The pain had stopped and the swelling was down visibly. Her fever had dropped and her complexion was normal. She was eating hungrily.

"No way you c'n get out, Slocum! Too many of us! We c'n starve you out!"

It was true. After tomorrow they would run out of food and there would be no way to get any. Slocum lit the kerosene lamp and hung it on its nail. Let them think he was still inside.

"Come out now," Mead said persuasively. "The easier you make it for us, the easier it'll be for you."

Slocum put the shotgun and the blanket in Pilar's arms. He carried her to the trap door and lowered her gently into the tunnel. He spread the blanket flat on the tunnel floor. He lowered her onto the blanket. Then he got in front and pulled the end of the blanket. She moved easily on the improvised travois.

At the river he placed her carefully on the ground. He

went back with the blanket. With infinite care he lowered the two boxes of dynamite onto the blanket. He wrapped the blanket around them and tied them together with heavy twine. The heavy wool blanket made good insulation. He doubled up some more twine and made a tow rope. He tugged the boxes carefully to the end of the tunnel. The sky outside was darkening rapidly.

He could hear Mead still bellowing into the megaphone. He saw Pilar tense when she heard Mead's voice. Mead was getting angrier since there was no response from the chapel. Finally he stopped. A few seconds later Choate took up the megaphone. His voice was calm and reasonable.

"Look here, Slocum," he said. "We know you're there. We've had our differences. I know you don't trust us. Don't blame you. You either starve to death with that nice lady or you come out, tell us where the treasure is, and we just let you go. Or you die. Which is it?"

Slocum turned the boat over and slid it into the reeds. He pulled the tree trunk close to the boat's port side and lashed it tightly to the hull by making several turns with the always-useful ball of twine. The long, level line of the gunwale was broken up by the twisted vertical and diagonal branches. In full darkness, the trunk drifting by should not attract attention. When Slocum could not see his hand held at full length in front of his face, he put Pilar in the boat. At the other end he carefully set the boxes of dynamite in their wool padding. He placed the hand-carved oars into the boat.

He waded into the river, pulling the boat after him. When it was afloat he stepped inside, knelt down, and took one oar. Using it as a paddle he moved the boat-tree craft diagonally across the river until it was close to the other shore. He quietly pulled the oar inside and laid it flat. Water was pouring into the boat through the open seams. It covered the bottom to a depth of two inches. It soaked Pilar's shirt and pants. It was rising much too rapidly.

When the boat had moved parallel to Mead's position a flick of the current caught the stern of the boat and slewed it around. Slocum cursed silently. This put the boat so that it was now drifting stern first. The tree camouflage was now on the side away from the five men. Slocum was too close to risk using the oar to correct their heading.

"What you keep lookin' at that goddamn boat for?" Mead suddenly demanded. "I hired you to keep a sharp lookout for Slocum. Forget the goddamn boat!"

Joe Charley's head was constantly in motion. Now it was fixed on the boat. His head swiveled scanning everything that came within its range. His eyes were now locked onto the boat. Joe Charley paid no attention to Mead's order. He stood up for a better view.

"Gentlemen," Choate said, "let me end this discussion."

He fired from his hip. The heavy bullet entered the boat just above the waterline and exited on the other side. Pilar had just raised both her knees and the bullet passed under them. Slocum's hand reached for his Colt and closed around the butt.

The current sent the boat close to shore. There the trunk snagged its branches on another beached driftwood branch. If Slocum tried to push it off, he knew the alert man would see the movement.

"That's funny," Joe Charley said slowly.

"What's funny?" Mead demanded. "Boat got snagged on a piece of driftwood."

"Somethin' funny," Joe Charley said. "Looks like that driftwood snagged itself a boat. Wish I knew someone who wanted a boat. I could get twenty, thirty dollars for a boat like that."

"Pack it on your head to Yuma, Joe Charley," Mead

said. Yuma was two hundred miles away across waterless desert. "And good luck."

Joe Charley turned to stare at him. "Mr. Mead," he said, "I am just about finished listenin' to you."

Good, good, thought Slocum. *Shoot each other, you bastards, and save me the trouble.* The men's voices carried well across the water.

"Forget the boat, everyone," Choate said. "It's not worth a plugged nickel any more with that hole I put in it. I'd like this meeting to come to order."

Even Mead laughed.

Joe Charley didn't like to see the boat ruined, even if he had never seriously planned to take it. It was a pointless kind of waste that he disliked, even though he would kill without compunction. A good boat took too long to build and required a craftsman, whereas any awkward fool could make a human being.

"You shit," Joe Charley said.

A sudden silence fell upon the group.

Shoot, shoot, Slocum prayed.

Mead said, "I think it's time you went an' scouted a bit, Joe Charley, 'cause I'm gettin' real tired of you."

Joe Charley was silent. Then he came to a decision. "Sure," he said. He stood up, climbed the bank, and walked in the darkness toward the mission.

"Touchy bastard," Mead said to no one in particular.

Slocum carefully began to unhook the branches of his camouflage tree from the driftwood ashore. One of the dried branches snapped. Slocum froze.

"What the hell's *that?*" Mead said.

"Current's pullin' that goddamn boat loose, is all," Sam Hart said.

The boat and its accompanying tree drifted loose. Then

the current took hold and swept them into the darkness.

Two hundred feet away, the sharp ears of Joe Charley had heard the branch crack. His hunting instinct took over. He stopped moving. The boat drifting with its tree was a coincidence, Joe Charley had decided. But when the noise from the breaking branch was added, it became too much. The current ran slowly. It did not run strongly enough to pull the boat away with such violence that a branch would snap.

Someone's in that boat, Joe Charley thought. When Choate fired at it and no sound came from it, Joe Charley had been sure it was empty. That was very clever of whoever was in the boat. When the branch cracked, Joe Charley was sure someone was in it. And the man in it had to be Slocum. Who the hell else would try to camouflage himself floating down the river? The man couldn't ride out on horseback. He knew he was surrounded. He must have found a secret tunnel. A lot of the missions in *Apacheria* had escape tunnels.

So it was Slocum.

Joe Charley turned around and walked to his horse. The camouflaged boat was now several hundred yards downstream and moving as fast as a man could walk.

"Hey, hey!" Mead called. "Where the hell are you goin'?"

Joe Charley said nothing.

"You leave now an' you don't get a goddamn penny!"

"Let me talk to 'im," Choate said in Mead's ear.

Joe Charley's hearing was exceptional. He yelled, "Go to hell, Choate! I know where Slocum is. You stay right there, you bunch o' culls an' I'll get 'im for you!"

Their voices carried well across the water. Slocum could just hear them. He had to abandon the boat and send it down the river as a decoy. He paddled the boat ashore. Working as fast as he could, he set Pilar ashore, removed the dynamite, then shoved the boat out into the current. It slid out into the river and moved slowly away into the darkness.

"The son of a bitch knows what he's talkin' about," Mead said. "We better foller."

In that country Slocum could do nothing without horses. And now there was his chance to get them. He bent down and whispered, "I'll be back." He turned and ran as fast as he could to the south, where the river had turned the flat land on both sides to lush pasture. There were no stones to impede his running. The grass was knee-high and made no barrier. He ran the half-mile in five minutes.

No one was watching the horses. They had been left saddled. Slocum took the two best ones and a packhorse. He led them quietly across the river, then mounted one. When he came to Pilar he boosted her gently into the saddle, and lashed the two boxes of dynamite onto the back of the packhorse.

Soon enough, Slocum knew, the tracker would realize he had been following a false trail. He would promptly go back and examine both sides of the river with expert precision. And Joe Charley would pick up their trail very quickly. So Slocum's best chance was to get up into the mountains. On flat desert country their chances of survival were too small. There was no place to hide, no good cover, no water, no food.

The mountains would give them all of that. They had to move as fast as they could till they reached high ground. It would be agony for Pilar's leg, but it had to be done.

He shook out two hundred feet of twine for the packhorse. If it fell with the dynamite that two hundred feet would be useful.

"Ready?"

Pilar knew what the fast trotting would do to her leg. She nodded bleakly.

"Let's go," Slocum said.

16

Joe Charley kept pace with the boat in the darkness. The river was too wide and the banks too low for him to see into the boat. He was wary of making any aggressive move until he knew exactly what he was facing. He was not stupid. Daylight would give him the knowledge he needed.

Mead and the others followed. Their horses moved at a walk in the darkness. After half an hour Mead said, "When is the son of a bitch gonna *do* somethin'?"

"Don't let him hear you call him that," Choate said. "He's got ears like a lynx."

"I'd like to tell that son of a bitch to go to hell," Mead said, but this time he lowered his voice. "But ain't none of us c'n walk decent yet. Ah, Christ! I'm gettin' tired of this."

"We're not going to push Joe Charley to speed up," Choate said. "If he makes a mistake he's dead. And if he's dead, there goes our chance at Slocum. And that's what I want more than anything else, Mead. I guess you want that, too?"

"I'm jus' plain tired o' talkin'." He turned around and looked at Hart and Clay. They were riding on the two packhorses Slocum had left them. "Look at 'em! Nothin' on their minds 'cept drinkin' an' screwin'. Look at 'em. Half asleep in the saddle. An you an' me, we're the big brains behind this here campaign. I'm beginnin' to feel like an idjit. My feet hurt, I'm tired an' sleepy, an' if this trail pisses out by mornin', I'm quittin', Choate. I'm tellin' you right now."

Choate looked at him and said nothing. They rode on in silence. The saddles creaked in the stillness above the soft padding of their horses' hooves through the meadow grass. When the grass ended the desert began. Then the clicking of stones under their horses became the dominant sound. They had moved into the chaparral.

Light leaked down from the eastern ridge. The boat drifted with the current, still attached to its driftwood camouflage. Now Joe Charley could see how Slocum had rigged the dirftwood to the boat. He smiled his wolfish grin and nodded in admiration. Joe Charley had his carbine resting across his horn, ready to fire. Ahead a low bluff rose thirty feet above the river. He rode up and dismounted. His horse would not stand still for fire. He dropped the reins and went flat. His carbine pointed at the boat. He waited for it to come under his observation. When it did, it was very little surprise to him that it was empty. He did not waste any time on regrets. He had played it carefully. He wanted to live a long time.

So Slocum had abandoned the boat sometime during the night. All Joe Charley had to do was pick up the trail. He stood up, mounted, and shoved the carbine back into its scabbard. He rode back.

"Well? Mead asked.

Everyone was yawning. They clustered around him. They hadn't shaved or taken a bath for two days. Typical of white men, Joe Charley thought. Indians bathed as frequently as possible wherever there was enough water.

Moreover, if the wind was right, a good tracker could smell an unwashed white man at quite a distance. Although Joe Charley was Mexican, he had so identified with his Apache companions that he considered himself an Indian.

"Gonna go back 'n' pick up the trail," he said briefly. He dismounted, pulled off his boots, and stripped naked.

"An' you're gonna take a *bath? Now?*" Mead asked in amazement. "I never seen nothin' like that before. *Never.*"

Joe Charley washed. He took a handful of sand and scrubbed himself. Satisfied, he rolled up his clothes and boots and lashed them to the saddle.

"Well, ain't you cute," Sam Hart said. Without turning around, Joe Charley reached inside his shirt. Both of Hart's hands were resting on his saddle horn. "I declare," Hart went on, "he's jus' about—"

A knife appeared in the horn. Joe Charley had pulled it from the sheath sewn into the neck of his shirt and flicked it expertly.

"Can I have it back?" Joe Charley asked politely.

Sam was so startled he pulled the knife out without a word and handed it over.

Joe Charley replaced the knife and said, "Soon's I cut his trail I'll signal. Best place is on the other side. I'll cross over an' go look. You gents will jus' have to git your feet wet. I dunno, mebbe a couple of you is actually gonna take a bath. Wouldn't hurt you none; you all smell like pregnant Digger squaws."

No one spoke. Joe Charley swam across with his horse. He mounted without looking at them. He began to move slowly upriver. His eyes searched for any sign of a trail.

"Shit," Mead said, in a bored, disgusted tone. He turned his horse and began keeping pace. The others followed, yawning or half dozing in the saddle.

But Joe Charley was excited. He knew he would cut Slocum's trail sometime that morning.

"We need sleep," Slocum said. He had almost fallen from the saddle. Pilar too, was swaying with fatigue. She absolutely had to rest. Exhaustion would not do her leg any good.

The danger was that he might oversleep. He would allow himself four hours. In that time Joe Charley would cut his trail and start pursuit, but Slocum figured he could get far enough in front to use his mountain knowledge.

"I need water and grass for the horses while we sleep. Keep a sharp lookout." In a few minutes she had spotted a tiny box canyon to the right. Inside, water trickling down the rock face formed a small pool, and also encouraged a dense stand of grass. The opening to the canyon was six feet wide and shrouded with mesquite. Slocum was so sleepy he hadn't noticed it, but her sharp eyes had seen the trickle of water down the rock. The narrow gap extended fifty feet. Heavily fissured granite rose 150 feet in the air.

Beyond the narrow entrance gap the canyon expanded suddenly like a bottle. The walls were vertical everywhere. There was only one entrance—and the exit was the entrance. It was a natural corral. All it needed was a gate six feet wide. But it would also be a death trap for anyone caught inside.

Inside, he staked the packhorse so that it could not get too near the others. Sometimes horses had arguments which they settled with kicks, and a sharp hoof smashing into a box of old dynamite . . . Solcum did not want to think about it. He kept the riding horses saddled.

"How can we be sure we'll wake up in time?" she asked with a worried frown.

"Indian alarm clock," he said with a grin.

She fell asleep immediately. The swelling had gone down. Slocum drank from the pool until his stomach couldn't hold any more water. In just under four hours he woke up. He had to relieve himself. The pressure of all the water he had drunk had forced him awake. It was an old Apache trick for exhausted warriors on a fast-moving war party. Frontiersmen called the technique the Indian alarm clock.

The sound of his movements woke her up. With her face averted she asked, "Indian alarm clock?"

"Indian alarm clock."

She laughed. "My leg feels better!" she said happily. She stood up and tested it. "But now I'm hungry."

They mounted and rode out. He noticed that the rock walls in the entrance seemed very unstable. A minor earth tremor and the beautiful box canyon would be lost forever. The packhorse trailed them dutifully at a safe distance.

Joe Charley grunted with satisfaction. He had found Slocum's footprints going into the river across from the hidden tunnel. Then he found the hoofprints of the three horses going up the bank. He stared with a puzzled expression. He recognized the hoofprints of the packhorse. The horse was carrying something which was too bulky to be carried in

saddlebags. It had to be something Choate and Mead wanted
very much. He had never been convinced of Mead's story
that they wanted to catch Slocum in order to get even. Seeing
the tracks of the packhorse had made it very clear to Joe
Charley. He was being used the way the Chinese fishermen
used cormorants when they went fishing. The cormorant
catches the fish, then the fisherman makes it give up the
fish.

"Well, I'm no goddamn Chinese bird," Joe Charley said
aloud. "I'd like a nice big swaller myself."

He waited for the men to catch up. He wanted a talk
with Mead about changing his pay schedule.

Slocum bent over, grabbed a bunch of mesquite pods, and
pulled. The bunch came off.

"They're good to eat," he said.

Pilar was famished but wary.

"Here, look," he said. He crunched a few. It had a pleas-
ant, nut-like flavor. She began munching. Her face suddenly
lit up. Slocum next looked for the beaver-tail shape of the
nopal cactus. He found some on a rocky outwash from a
low, V-shaped pass. He snapped off a dry mesquite branch,
sharpened it with his jackknife, and speared one of the nopal
pods. He picked up a handful of grass, rolled it into a ball,
and brushed off the spines.

He handed the nopal to her. "Chew it and spit out the
seeds," he told her. The flesh was red and filled with black
seeds. She chewed with enjoyment after the first tentative
bite.

"Your people taught me what's good to eat in the desert,"
he said.

Her face flushed and she averted her head. Slocum cursed
himself for his stupidity. Her people had discarded her like

garbage. A white man had brought her up.

"You do not understand," she said sharply. "My mother must have loved me. She had to desert me or I might have infected all the rest. And all would have died. I hate the white man who brought this disease with him when he came here."

"Hate?"

She flushed. "I beg God for his pardon. It is the weakness of my spirit which made me say that."

They rode in silence. Slocum turned every few minutes and looked at their back trail. They always climbed upward. He was looking for favorable ground to defend. A cave with a water supply and a narrow path leading to it that would be ideal. They'd spend a few days trying to seize it from Slocum. Then would come the realization that any frontal attack would end in a few deaths. And then Sam and George would say the hell with it and rebel. Choate would become philosophical about it and leave a little while later. But Mead would hang on like a grim snapping turtle to the very end.

But even if Mead would finally give up in disgust— since everyone except Joe Charley would have pulled out— that would still leave Joe Charley.

Slocum could smell the hunter there. Slocum was that way himself, so he recognized it right away in someone else. Slocum wanted to kill his pursuers and end this irritating chase. He had no doubt at all that, left to himself, he could do it. But first he would kill Joe Charley.

With their hunting falcon gone the others, with their damaged feet, would be somewhat less of a problem for Slocum. He would get them one by one.

The big problem was Pilar.

She would not permit it. And he had promised.

He sighed, then turned to scan the ledges, the mountain

slopes, the arroyo walls. Caves, if they were in shadow, would be invisible. If the sun were to shine directly inside there would be no way to judge depth, and consequently the cave would look just like the rest of the cliff face. If the sunlight hit at just the right angle it would cast a shadow keen eyes would notice.

His eyes never stopped moving. They skimmed across mountain slopes, examined their back trail, then looked at the sky to see if there were rain clouds boiling over a nearby mountain which would trigger a savage cloudburst and a ten-foot wall of water. A heave rain could plunge down one of the arroyos he had been planning to use for easy access to some ridge.

He never took a trail which would outline them against the sky. He did not want to make Joe Charley's work any easier for him. He always skirted a slope on its shoulder. Once around the ridge he would climb to the crest, go flat before he reached it, and scan his back trail.

The problem was that Joe Charley would know what Slocum was thinking. He would not display himself in daylight. He was very likely hanging back at each ridge until he was sure that Slocum had moved ahead.

Joe Charley hoped that Slocum would relax his guard, figuring his pursuers had given up, particularly if Slocum never caught sight of Joe Charley all day. Night would be the ideal time to take Slocum. Joe Charley did not know that Slocum knew he had joined the group. Joe Charley's logic was pretty good—but in Slocum he had met a mind aware of the subtleties of strategy.

Joe Charley halted. In a few minutes the others straggled along and stopped beside him.

"What's the matter now?" Mead growled. He shook his canteen. It was almost empty.

"Nothin'. Best to wait."

"Here? With no water? In the middle of the goddamn desert?"

When Joe Charley had been a scout with the Fifth Cavalry under Captain Lundberg, chasing White River Apaches under the Mogollon Rim, that experienced frontier officer had never questioned Joe Charley's judgment. When Joe Charley, for instance, said "We camp here," Captain Lundberg just nodded and gave the necessary orders. When Joe Charley lifted his head and sniffed the air like a coyote out hunting and said "Stop here. Go on foot," the captain knew his scout had smelled something important. He might say, "Sure, Joe Charley, what's up?" And Joe Charley might say he had smelled roasting mescal far up a canyon; the cool descending air signaled that only Apache women were there.

Captain Lundberg might say, "Suggestion, Joe Charley?" And the scout would say, "Capture women. Hold prisoners till men come in to Fort Apache and surrender and sign treaty."

"Good idea, Joe Charley," Captain Lundberg would say, with a broad smile. It worked out just fine. Captain Lundberg said civilian scouts couldn't get medals, so with his own money he bought a beautiful Winchester carbine and gave it to Joe Charley.

And now these filthy sons of bitches were asking him all sorts of stupid questions. He was getting sick of them. He would have walked away from them the day before but he kept thinking of the pretty whore who wanted that ring. He guessed he would stay one more day. And he wasn't sure what he would do if Mead started up again.

"'Cause I say we stop," Joe Charley said.

Choate recognized a man who would not be pushed one step further.

Mead's face darkened. Choate knew the type. Mead was

a man who had to challenge every statement not in perfect agreement with his own ideas.

Choate said mildly, "Joe Charley, what's your reason?"

Joe Charley liked Choate's tone. It was a lot like Captain Lundberg's style.

"Slocum knows we're follerin'."

"How?" Mead immediately challenged.

"If he's as smart as you say he is, he *knows*. So he's waitin' for us to show up out there." Joe Charley waved his hand. "An' when he does that, he c'n pick his spot. *I* want to pick the spot. I'm pickin' it t'night. Then I'll take 'im."

"Wait a minute here," Mead said. *"I* want 'im. I'm the man gonna chew 'im up an' spit 'im out. You're the feller we hired to trail 'im, is all. You got that clear?"

"Well, shit," Joe Charley said. That was the last straw. "I quit." *And there*, he thought, *there goes the ring for the little whore in Benson*.

"You go an' I ain't payin' you a goddamn cent!"

Joe Charley said indifferently, "Put my money on a red-hot spoon an' shove it up your ass, Mead."

Sam laughed. Mead punched him in the face. Sam went over sideways in the saddle but regained his balance. His hand dropped to his gun butt, but Choate jammed his horse between him and Mead.

"Don't do it, Sam! We'll all wind up shooting each other and Slocum will laugh his head off when he finds out. I mean, first he takes our boots, now we're pulling on each other."

Mead had one of his sudden mood changes. "Yeah," he said. "Lost my head. Sorry, Sam. Shake on it?"

Sam shook hands. He liked and respected Mead. His honor had demanded that he shoot, but he was terrified at

Mead's speed and brilliance with a gun.

Choate sighed as he watched the reconciliation. He was sorry he had ever started on the whole Slocum deal. But it was too late to back out now.

They watched Joe Charley ride toward Tucson.

"Dirty half-breed son of a bitch," Mead said.

"I'm not worried," Choate said. "It's four of us against one man and a goddamn woman. We'll get 'em tomorrow."

Losing the ring did not end Joe Charley's interest in Slocum.

Now his sole motivation was his pride. Slocum's mind intrigued Joe Charley. He recognized in Slocum his own kind of hawk's mind and sharpness of perception.

As he rode he kept thinking about this. And after an hour he swung his horse's head to the right. He had decided to get Slocum on his own, for the sheer pleasure of the game. He had no desire to torture Slocum. He might take the girl, but it depended upon how difficult it was with Slocum. Maybe he would kill her afterwards if she put up too much of a fight or bit him.

He knew Mead would still go after Slocum. Very likely he wouldn't wait till morning. But men like Mead didn't really know how to make time on horseback. He would push a horse till it dropped, then buy or steal another one and keep going.

Joe Charley knew horses. It was hard, for instance, for a horse to go all day with a man on his back who weighed 180 pounds. A horse needed to rest with all that weight on him. And the best way to rest a horse and still make time was simple: walk.

So Joe Charley dismounted every fifteen minutes and walked for fifteen minutes. Then he rode again for fifteen minutes, then walked again.

Mead and the others never dismounted. They couldn't walk anyway, of course, not with their feet in such a condition, but even if they had been able to walk, they wouldn't have.

Far ahead was the range where Joe Charley was sure Slocum was hiding. He was right.

Slocum had found his impregnable position. He and Pilar had dismounted. They were sitting on a level bench set among junipers.

The horses were scrounging for whatever blades of grass they could find on the stony slopes. Slocum had found mescal. He pulled off the outer leaves and cut out the central stalks. He broke off some dead juniper branches and made a fire to bake the mescal. While it baked he stared into the hot embers and planned his next step.

Pilar could walk now. It was awkward, but she could walk. He heard her moving around in back of him while he looked intently over their back trail. They he turned around to see if Joe Charley had figured out Slocum's line of march and was sitting directly in his path to take him by surprise.

Pilar was behind him.

"Are you hungry?" Slocum asked her. He took the mescal out of the hot coals. "Eat," he said.

"I don't know how to eat it," she said.

Slocum had forgotten that she was only an Apache by birth.

"Chew it and spit out the fiber," he told her.

"All right," she said, and worked at it for a while.

"John?" she asked suddenly.

"Yes?"

"What shall we do? I am tired of running from these men."

"I have been thinking about what to do, Pilar. And now that your leg is better, we are going to do it."

Slocum made a wide sweep. What he wanted to do to end the pursuit and destroy the pursuers was to double back and head for the box canyon where they had watered. He would use the canyon as a bait to lure in the rats. Then he would close the trap.

The idea was spectacular. It had come to him suddenly. He could only carry out his plan if he reached the canyon before they showed up on his trail. This had now become possible, although Slocum did not know it, because of the bickering among Joe Charley, Choate, and Mead.

If they had stuck to business and followed him swiftly his plan would not have had any chance of success.

Slocum moved at a fast trot. In three hours he had circled the mountain at the western end of which the box canyon was located. On the southern side an arroyo opened up. Slocum put the horses in there. The rain that had soaked in during the rainy season had produced lush grass. He unsaddled the horses and let them graze. A tiny trickle of water flowed along the stony center of the arroyo. After he and Pilar had drunk their fill he set out to scout. He saw where it would be possible to climb up to the cliff which hung over the narrow entrance to the box canyon. He smiled in satisfaction.

Pilar noticed. It was a cold smile. The only other time she had seen him smile like that was when he had put Mead and the others afoot.

"I think it will work," he told her.

He carefully unpacked the dynamite. Then he walked around to the western side until he had rejoined their old trail. He walked beside it. He was careful not to mingle his new tracks with their old ones.

What he wanted was to persuade Joe Charley that he and Pilar were still inside the box canyon. And the second part of his plan would ensure that the scout would not think it was a trap to lure him inside. Slocum wanted Joe Charley and the others to go in without doing anything smart like climbing the mountain first for a quick look-see. He had to do something to make them drop that elementary precaution.

While he was thinking of a good way to bait the trap he had walked three hundred yards past the canyon opening. He reached out and broke off a mesquite branch. With the branch he traced his steps and erased all signs of his and Pilar's earlier passage. When he reached the box canyon opening it would seem, even to an experienced tracker like Joe Charley, that their three horses had turned into the canyon and were still there.

Crawling backwards, he carefully brushed out all signs of his second trail. About a hundred feet before the entrance to the canyon he heard the familiar buzzing of a diamondback sounding its warning.

It was a big one, as big as the the rattler which had struck Pilar. It was coiled under a creosote bush just beside the trail. If it had not sounded its warning Slocum would have backed right into it.

He stood and stared at it. Unlike most other diamond-backs, it did not quietly flow away. It stood its ground. Its black tongue flickered back and forth like forked lightning. Maybe it was a female and had some eggs in a ground squirrel's burrow nearby.

The unblinking yellow eyes in the big arrow-shaped head stared at him. The big poison sacs gave the head its distinctive V-shape. If it had no luck hunting it would be carrying plenty of venom. If it had bitten him—

Slocum gave a low cry of triumph. He knew how to lure Joe Charley into the canyon.

17

Sam Hart said, "I gotta piss."

No one paid any attention. He slid out of the saddle, groaned as his battered feet touched the ground. After he relieved himself he remounted and caught up with the others. The four of them had been pushing their horses to the limit. The horses were lathered with foam. Strings of saliva hung from their mouths. Ordinarily Choate would not have done such a thing to his horse, but he had been caught up in Mead's wild, delirious passion to avenge himself because of Slocum's blow to his pride.

Choate said, "If these nags die on us, we're next, Mead. I don't see walking across sixty miles of desert. We're not going to meet a peddling man with a barrel of cold water and sandwiches, not this time."

Mead stood in his stirrups with a painful grunt. He had just seen something moving across the chaparral flats. Then he sank back. "My," he said, "I do declare I've jus' seen our friend what quit on us. Mr. Joe Charley himself!"

Choate and the others stood in their stirrups. It was true. Mead held up his hand. They stopped.

"Let's see if I c'n figger this. Joe Charley has got lost? I doubt it. Or Joe Charley is lookin' to get Slocum an' see what makes 'im tick. I don' think he buys our story at all, Choate."

"I agree."

"An' if he don' believe it, what does he believe?"

"I believe he wants to talk to Slocum himself. Privately."

"'Privately,'" Mead repeated with a sneer. "I c'n see you was brought up in a real nice fam'ly. They send you to a fancy college like Harvard?"

Choate had gone to West Point. He had been commissioned as a second lieutenant, fought well in the Civil War, and come out a major. Stationed in Texas, he had killed a fellow officer in a drunken argument. Because of his record, the charge was reduced to manslaughter on the condition that he resign. He did so, and had been wandering across the West ever since.

"No, Mr. Mead. I, like you, never got past the first grade."

Sam choked with laughter. Choate was in no mood for the childish chatter with which Mead always strove to assert his dominance.

"If we've seen Joe Charley," Choate went on, "he's seen us. Right?"

"Yeah," Mead growled.

"So we had better team up with him again. We need him to scout for us. We need him for places where climbing on foot might be necessary. And believe me, Mr. Mead, it will be."

He pointed to the harsh line of mountains ahead.

"Slocum's smart," he continued. "He knows he's got a lot of advantages, being in the mountains."

Whenever Choate's speech was attacked he responded with even more precision of speech. That way, whoever had made the remark was continually forced to realize how poorly he spoke English. The procedure usually worked. Mead clearly resented the upper-class accent and diction flowing from Choate in a calm, faintly contemptuous tone.

"So," Choate summed up, "it behooves us to be friendly."

Mead said nothing. Choate took his silence for assent. He spurred ahead and waved his sombrero. Then he rode his horse back and forth in the plains signal that meant, *I want to talk.*

Slocum pulled his Colt and blew the diamondback's head to pieces. The coils, thick around as a man's calf, jerked and quivered for a full minute. When it finally stopped Slocum found himself admiring the beautiful diamond pattern and the way it broke up light and shadow so that if the snake were motionless it was hard to make out its outline.

He stepped up to the creosote bush under which it had been coiled and deliberately pissed on the bush. He sat down next to the bush and lay back. He took out his jackknife and clenched his left fist tightly until the vein in his wrist became prominent. He carefully nicked the edge of the vein. Blood poured out. He directed several tablespoons of it onto the ground close to the dead snake.

Joe Charley was sure to examine this area with the utmost care. If Slocum could convince Joe Charley, then the others would automatically go along with their scout's decision.

The picture Slocum was painting for Joe Charley couldn't be clearer. Slocum had stopped to take a leak. He had dismounted and stepped up to the creosote bush. As he was pissing, the big diamondback struck. Slocum shot the snake. Then he had sat down and made the incisions at the fang marks with his jackknife. He was nervous because of the rattler's huge size. He had made the cuts too big—perfectly believable, because even the bravest men were terrified of being bitten. It was too hot to lie in the open and recuperate or wait to see what would happen. There was a box canyon just ahead. Joe Charley would think that Slocum knew about it and had headed for it immediately, for its shade and water.

And there he was holed up. He would be either dead or in a bad way. The woman would be there, too, but she knew little about guns.

All Joe Charley had to do was take a walk into the canyon. A little normal vigilance was all that would be necessary, and there his prey would be, dying from a diamondback bite. Neat.

Slocum walked to the trail and then back again. His agitated movements would conceal the fact that, in reality, the horses had never stopped here.

Any feeling Joe Charley might have that something was not quite correct would be overruled by the enormous dead snake and all the blood.

Slocum imagined Joe Charley putting it all together. Indeed, Slocum himself might fall for it if the situation had been reversed.

Satisfied at last, he moved off the old trail. Crawling backwards, he brushed out his most recent tracks. He fervently hoped that he wouldn't be backing into another diamondback, but he did not.

The next thing he had to do was to prepare the welcoming

party. This had to be designed around Pilar's strict rule, *Do Not Kill*. It was not easy to obey that and still be able to protect both of them from further pursuit.

But now he had found a way.

He found a crevice in the rock face where the sun could not penetrate. He left Pilar there with a canteen of water and several ripe mesquite pods. She could survive on it. Her people had done so for centuries.

He left her the Colt. There might be another snake or a hydrophobic skunk. And if one of the men stumbled into her, she could make her own choice about her philosophy of killing. Because Slocum would have to be away from her for at least one day, maybe two. It depended on how fast they were being trailed. He would need as much light as possible when he began to climb with those two boxes of dynamite on his back. He could not afford a slip in the darkness. He pulled the Winchester from its saddle scabbard. With a short length of his reata he made an acceptable sling. To carry the boxes he used the old technique developed by men who had to carry heavy weights.

He lashed the two boxes together with a vertical tie around both boxes. He set the boxes on top of a flat rock. He backed up to the rock and ran another length of the reata from the front of the boxes to the rear, then around to the front again. He took the two loose ends of the reata, pulled them around his shoulders, and twisted the ends tightly together twice. He squatted a bit, and then stood up. The boxes rode easily on his back. His thighs took all the weight.

If he were to find himself suddenly losing his balance because of a stone that might shift under his foot as he climbed up he would not have to fall backwards with his load and be scattered all across the mountainside.

All he had to do was open the hand that held the ends

of the reata together. The two turns would spin in a fast unwind and the load would drop free. Hopefully, it would land far below. If that happened, he would press his body flat against the rock and cover the back of his head with his hands.

Time to go. He took a long drink of water from his canteen and began to climb.

"That half-breed fuck is join'in us,", Mead said.

Choate looked at him.

"All right, Choate, I ain't gonna say it as long's he's in the same county. Satisfied?"

"Yes."

They stopped and waited until Joe Charley rode up. He said nothing. Mead nodded. Joe Charley nodded, but his nod was just a trifle shorter than Mead's. Mead flushed. He wanted to show that he was willing to be friendly, but that bastard Mexican wanted to win at everything he did.

"Como 'sta?" asked Choate.

"Bien, bien. We got the deal goin' again?"

"Yeah, I suppose," Mead said grudgingly.

"You really been pushin' hard, ain't cha?" Joe Charley said, looking at their horses.

"Come to the point," Mead said. He could not refrain from responding to any criticism.

"Point is, you push them horses for half an hour more like you been doin', an' you all are gonna have to start hoofin' it all over again, Mead."

Mead started to tell him it was none of his business but Choate said, "All right. What about *their* horses?"

"Not much better'n yours, looks like. They're takin' shorter 'n' shorter steps. Hardly no grass the way they've come, *poco agua.* They gotta find both fast. So they're headin' for the mountains."

Mead didn't like to hunt people in the mountains. Mountains hid your enemy too well. Ambushes were too easy. Shoot at someone from a high position and then try to get to him—it could take half a day. And by then the son of a bitch could be half a county away.

"How's our chances of catchin' 'em before they get there?"

"If you fellers knew how to handle horses, pretty good. The way you push 'em, no."

Mead hated to be told he was in any way incompetent. "I don' think you know what you're talkin' about, Joe Charley. An' that's the honest-to-God truth, if you wanna know."

"I don' wanna know," Joe Charley said simply.

Sam couldn't resist a short bark of laughter.

"What's your suggestion, Joe Charley?" Choate asked, with a sigh. He was getting tired of defusing dangerous situations constantly being created by Mead. His consolation was that everything would end in a day or two days, at the most.

"I follow," Joe Charley said. "When I got 'em, I'll stay an' watch till you come up. If they move again I'll follow—"

"But you don' do any shootin'! That clear?"

"*Claro.* But s'ppose they shoot at me, *patrón?*"

He spoke the word for "boss" without any sarcasm in his voice, but the faint smile at the corners of his lips was calculated to force Mead's temperature to soar.

"Jus' fall back an' wait for us, Joe Charley. An' that's an order from the *patrón. Claro?*"

"Yeah. Sure. I fall back. Sure."

Even Choate had to smile at the dry sarcasm of that remark.

How could you ask a falcon to release a rabbit in its talons if the rabbit kicked it?

"Jus' ride easy," Joe Charley said, "Mebbe you'll be able

to walk a li'l bit, if you gotta. *Adios*." He lifted a hand in farewell, grinned, and moved off at a trot.

"Knows his business," Choate said. Some day when he was planning a big operation he'd like to bring Joe Charley in on it. A man like him was worth three ordinary ones. He watched as Joe Charley kept turning his head to left and right. He would *never* ride into an ambush. He had too many feelers out all the time. A man could feel confident with Joe Charley around.

It was a strain working with these half-insane ex-Quantrill men. They should have moved to Brazil after the War like so many other rebels, rather than live under the despised flag of the Union. If only they had gone, Choate thought, maybe he wouldn't be riding an exhausted, thirsty horse across this goddamned cactus desert.

Well, we'd only be with them for a day or two more. He could stand that much, although it would be a strain.

18

Slocum's problem was to get on the cliff overhang above the narrow entrance to the box canyon.

At the right moment all he had to do was to push both boxes over the edge. The crystallized nitroglycerin would explode instantly. The heavily fissured granite would do all the rest when the massive explosion reached it.

There was a risk that the top of the cliff on which he would be standing would collapse too, but it was a good risk. Slocum had been in worse situations—though not much worse.

The bottom of the slope was covered with talus, rock fragments which had weathered downward from the higher slopes through water freezing and expanding in the fissures higher up.

Slipping and sliding and catching his balance with his

free hand, tense with exertion and from apprehension, Slocum slowly forged upward. After he had passed three hundred feet of the loose talus which had come to rest at its thirty-degree angle of repose, he came to a steeper gradient.

Then he realized that his boots would have to come off. Very gently he backed up to a relatively level stretch. He set down his load gingerly, pulled off his boots, tied them onto the load, and packed up again.

The grade was steeper now, but his stockinged feet held far better than boot leather. Step by step he crawled up. The struggle was worse because there was nowhere to set down his load for a rest. The angle was too steep for him to be able to pick it up again. Eating a few bunches of mesquite beans was good enough for a man traveling on horseback. It was not good enough for a man climbing a mountain, hoisting his own body weight as well as sixty pounds of dynamite.

His stockings began to fray, and then to tear on the stones. Little cuts formed on his soles. He began to bruise his feet on rocks he could not see because his attention had to be carefully focused directly ahead and not on the stones he was about to step on.

So this kind of bootless walking was what Mead and Choate had to face. The thought made him smile. At least they had done it on level desert, and without carrying a load. He risked a quick look up. It seemed that he had been walking on a treadmill and hadn't moved at all. His face was dripping with sweat. It ran into his eyes and made them sting. He had left his sombrero behind. He was sorry he had not made himself a sweatband from the tail of his shirt.

He opened his mouth wide and pumped in more oxygen. His legs pumped up and drove downward, pumped up again and drove downward. If he were to try to avoid sharp stones it seemed to Slocum that it would take years to reach the top.

The trick was to pay no attention to the pain and keep moving. For that a man had to send his mind somewhere far away from his body. If his mind stayed in his body, it would worry about what was happening to his feet.

So he sent it back to Nuestra Señora de los Rios, to the cemetery in back of the chapel, where lay the gold candlesticks, the rose pearls, the rubies, and the emeralds on the Virgin's robe.

His mind made a rough count of what all of that would bring when sold. He knew a magnificent ranch in northern California, one hundred miles northeast of San Francisco. It had lakes and streams and heavy woods. He could even grow grapes and make his own wine if he wanted; the rancher's widow wanted to sell it and go back to live in Boston.

Suddenly Slocum was at the top.

He slowly sank into a kneeling position. Very, very carefully he let the boxes slide down till they were solidly on the level rock. He unslung the carbine and set it beside the boxes. He unscrewed his canteen and drank half of the contents.

Never had water tasted so good. His shirt and pants were soaked with sweat. His stockings were in bloody shreds. He pulled on his boots over the swollen flesh. Just in time, he figured. Another ten minutes and he'd be worse off than Mead and his men had been on their desert walk.

It was only when Chato came to the fresh tracks that he stopped abruptly. Then he spun around and went flat. He crawled quickly in absolute silence. He was a skilled warrior of thirty-six years, and was on the war trail by himself because he disliked the war chief the others were following.

He carried a bow and a quiver of arrows. In his pouch was a rusty, fire-blackened Colt which he had removed from the ashes of a lonely ranch house. He had no bullets for it.

He counted three horses. A man was sleeping in the shade of the cliff. The other two had gone. He did not know that the person he thought was a sleeping man was Pilar.

One pair of boot tracks led out. Where was the third man? He puzzled over this for a while. His black war paint began to melt and run in streaks. Once more he counted three horses grazing, and only two saddles. His black eyes restlessly swept the terrain and then he noticed the pack-saddle.

Good! The third horse, then, was a packhorse. That meant there were only two men. One set of boot tracks led out; that puzzled him. None of the horses seemed crippled.

The man rolled in his sleep. Just beyond the sleeping figure's right elbow was a Colt in its holster. And the gunbelt was full of cartridges.

His heart jumped. Doshay, the war chief with whom he had fought over a woman, had a fine Colt which he had taken from a cavalry lieutenant below Mule Creek. He was always boasting about the Colt and making fun of Chato's useless gun.

Here was his chance. He took off his bow and quiver. The best thing to do would be to come within striking distance, and then go for the man's throat with his knife.

Then he would saddle the best horse and lead out the other two. When he was a safe distance away he could kill the packhorse and broil himself a steak over mesquite wood, which, like juniper, made no smoke.

It looked like a good day. He pulled his knife.

* * *

Slocum panted. There was absolutely no shade. The sun blazed off the rock and reflected the savage desert heat. He had left his sombrero below. He knotted his bandanna at the corners and put it on his head. He sipped some water, rolled it around in his mouth, and spit it back into the canteen.

Once more he wondered what might happen if the cliff were to collapse under him.

After he had pushed the dynamite over he would have about four seconds to move away from the edge. And on high-heeled boots, with bleeding and bruised feet. He spent the next three hours creating a path clear of any rocks which might impede the progress of a man really bent on getting the hell out of there.

At least the project gave him something to do.

When he finished at last, he had made a smooth path sixty feet long. He could do sixty feet in four seconds in high-heeled boots. And if he thought he couldn't, the picture of himself falling with the dynamited cliff would give wings to his feet.

Chato was within fifteen feet of the sleeping Pilar. He slowly rose to a crouching position and prepared for the final rush.

She turned restlessly in her sleep. Chato saw her breasts under her unbuttoned shirt. He halted in amazement. A woman! His hand dropped to his side.

Suddenly he realized she was not a white woman. She was Apache. He slid the knife back into its sheath.

He bent down and touched her shoulder. "What are you doing here?" he asked angrily, in guttural Apache.

She stared at him without understanding.

"Why are you dressed like a man? With your hair cut like a man? That is not decent for an Apache woman!"

She shook her head.

He had never heard of an Apache who did not speak the language.

He stared at her in puzzlement for a few seconds. He had to find out where the other person was. He pointed to one of the saddles, then moved his forefinger to the trail left by Slocum. Then he looked at her with a question in his eyes.

She shrugged.

Chato spoke some Spanish and a little English. The Spanish he had picked up from his occasional contacts with the Mexicans in the Sierra Madre, the English from living on the reservation up near Fort Grant.

"Prisonero?"

"No."

"Mujer de un Americano?"

She shook her head. He began to look at her with admiration. This was a superb Apache woman. A bit old, perhaps, for a wife, but still young enough to bear many children and some strong warriors.

He waited patiently for an explanation. She told him briefly that she had been abandoned by her people when she was a baby, and that she had been saved and brought up by a Mexican holy man.

"There are some good white people," he admitted. He sat cross-legged and looked at Pilar. He did not know what to do with the woman any more. When was the white man coming back?

She did not know. Maybe tomorrow.

Why didn't he ride?

She didn't know. He was very good to her, she said. She showed Chato her still slightly puffed-up leg. She had been bitten by a big diamondback and he had saved her life. He was taking her back to Mexico, where she would live again with many other holy women.

Chato decided not to kill her. "Do you have something to eat?" he asked. She pointed to a few mesquite pods nearby.

He took half of them and munched them while he thought, *What breasts to suckle strong sons!*

19

Joe Charley's stare was fixed upon the wild confusion of hoof and boot marks in the trampled trail. His eyes followed the track to the right and saw the dead diamondback. His face grew thoughtful as he dismounted. When he saw the discolored soil where Slocum had bled he kneeled and smelled, with his nose almost touching the ground.

Blood. Lots of it. And he smelled human urine at the base of the creosote bush.

He stood up and carefully examined the trail again. The trail went straight for several hundred yards to the steep nearby mountain.

He mounted. The trail suddenly swerved into a canyon. He rode by with his carbine out and the butt resting on his right hip. He rode by the entrance quickly. Nothing stirred.

He rode back. He saw the far wall of the canyon; he

judged its distance at five hundred yards. Grass and water, that was sure.

Far above him Slocum looked down at Joe Charley. Slocum was very good with carbines and rifles. Here there was no windage to allow for. He could drop the man with one shot. With Joe Charley on the ground Slocum could finish him off at his leisure. But there was the matter of his promise to Pilar. He reluctantly laid the carbine down.

Joe Charley turned around and rode slowly back the way he had come. Slocum could read his mind as if his thoughts were printed on a page. He was like a rat that could smell the very tasty cheese inside. Was it a trap? He suddenly looked up. Slocum's head was well hidden. Joe Charley relaxed a bit. He rode back and forth, thinking hard.

Slocum turned to look at Joe Charley's back trail. About six miles away, as he estimated, he saw a dust cloud. Occasionally metal flashed: bridle bits and guns. Mead and Choate.

Joe Charley remained motionless for a minute. Then he rode to the edge of the mountain and looked.

He was thinking that all this pussyfooting around was a terrible waste of time if that wasn't really a box canyon, but just a narrow-necked entrance into a nice little pasture with another exit at the far side. Maybe Slocum and the woman had watered there; maybe, even though he had been badly bitten by that big diamondback, Slocum had decided to push ahead with her rather than risk their pursuers coming up to them.

It wouldn't hurt to spend maybe twenty minutes or so for a look-see at the other side of the mountain. No trail coming out of the box canyon would mean they were still inside. And if it *was* a box canyon, they were stuck inside with no way out.

And even if they should emerge from the canyon by the front door while Joe Charley was looking for the back door, Mead and Choate could get them.

Joe Charley abruptly started around to look at the other side of the mountain.

"Shit!" muttered Slocum. Pilar was there and there was no way he could warn her. If he did manage to get her attention, he could kiss his dynamite plan goodbye. She would never shoot. And he had promised her that he would not.

He would just have to break his promise. If Joe Charley spotted that cool recess in the cliff where she was resting— and he certainly would—then Slocum would shoot.

From his vantage point on the cliff top Slocum's last sight of Joe Charley would be when he started to ride into Pilar's resting place. Hitting him in the right shoulder would be best, since the chances were that the scout would be right-handed.

Slocum lay prone. He took his shirt off and rolled it into a ball and set it on a flat rock. With their short barrels, carbines were not designed for distance work. He would have to allow for a fast gravity drop of the bullet. The fabric would absorb the recoil.

But the wind was acting up down below. He could see a couple of the miniature tornadoes—dust devils—spinning across the desert floor. The brown cylinders were six feet tall, and they staggered in a haphazard fashion. A sudden gust could throw a bullet two or three inches from his aiming point—the center of Joe Charley's right shoulder blade. So, if the wind were acting up just as he squeezed the trigger, Joe Charley, if the bullet were forced to the left, would have a sear across his upper arm. If the wind gusted the other way, the bullet would enter his throat. That would be the end of Joe Charley. *And good riddance,* Slocum thought.

But suppose the bullet only seared him. Joe Charley would go flat, figure the shot came from up the mountain, and he'd know there was no way for whoever fired to get in another one before he'd be into the recess—alone with Pilar.

Nor could whoever it was who had fired at him—for he'd as yet have no idea that it was Slocum who had shot at him—get down from the mountain in less than three hours' time. Time enough to harm the woman. Time enough to ride out with the horses and warn Mead away from the box canyon entrance.

With four carbines waiting for Slocum's appearance, he had to be realistic. It looked plain bad. Slocum pressed his cheek against the smooth walnut stock of the Winchester and prayed for the wind to stop.

Chato had snared a rabbit. In ten minutes he had skinned and gutted it, lit a tiny smokeless fire, and was broiling it with a sharpened stick. A fine Apache woman like the one lying a quarter of a mile back should eat something better than mesquite beans.

Maybe if the white man didn't come back by tomorrow morning she would come with him. He would teach her the language of the People.

A horseman was coming. Chato had made his fire in a hollow among some saguaro. It was an area anyone walking or riding would automatically avoid. As soon as Chato had heard the horse coming across the hard-packed clay he froze. His brown skin blended perfectly with the brown of the desert floor. The saguaro branches broke up his outline.

Only an intense, slow, careful scrutiny would have revealed his existence. But Joe Charley was far too intent on looking for tracks coming out of the mountain to spend much time looking elsewhere.

Was this rider the woman's friend? He looked more Mexican. And if he knew where she was, why was he watching for tracks, instead of riding straight to her?

Chato put down the rabbit. He picked up his bow and selected two arrows from the quiver. He moved silently in the slight hollow just in back of the horseman, forty feet to his right.

Chato had practiced with the bow and arrow since he was four years old. At ranges up to sixty feet his accuracy was deadly.

"Where's the nearest water?" Mead demanded.

Choate had never been in this part of Arizona. He had never even seen a map of it. Low, dusty chaparral was everywhere.

"Back in Tucson," Choate said.

"Horses gotta water by t'night," Mead said, "or we're gonna have another goddamn hike in front of us. I don' fancy *that*. Not twice in a row."

"Mead, the laughing-stock of the Territory," Choate said.

The heat was so searing that there was no dampness on their skin. As soon the sweat reached the surface of the skin it evaporated immediately. As the water left their bodies their blood began to thicken with its loss. Thickened blood has to be forced through the arteries by a heart which has to work even harder than normal.

The smartest desert dwellers—coyotes, rabbits, snakes— all hole up during the hottest part of the day in order to conserve body moisture and strength. Choate thought about this.

"Mead," he said, "let's call a halt."

"What?"

"We're just about at the end of our rope. I'm not made for desert travel. Neither are you. Neither are the horses."

"What you talkin' about? You mean jus' *stop?*"

"Yes."

"What the hell good will that do, Choate? You're goin' loco in the heat." He jerked his chin at a scrubby little beavertail cactus. "You want us to rest in the shade of that there big, beautiful tree?"

Choate said patiently, "We tie our saddle blankets together. Tie the ends to cactus or mesquite. We have a tent. We just sit there till late afternoon. Save water, save sweating."

"We put the horses in with us, hey?" Mead sneered.

Choate tried to imagine what Mead's wife was like, if he had ever been married. She was either twice as bad as he was, or she was a terrified, silent rabbit.

"No. They stay outside," Choate said patiently. He would not respond to Mead's sarcasm. "But with their saddles off they'll at least get some rest. What d'you say, Mead?"

"I'll tell you what, Choate," Mead said. He rubbed his unshaven chin while he pretended to deliberate. "I tell you, it's a good idea if we was mappin' this here county and gettin' paid by the day. But we ain't. I got only a few dollars left, an' what we're after is only a little ways ahead. I don' wanna take it easy. As for bein' thirsty, I been thirsty before. I c'n stand it, an' so c'n my boys.

"An' I don' give a shit about the horses," he continued. "They c'n stand a few more hours of this. Because t'night the hull dang shebang is gonna be over—finished!

"So if you wanna cry like an old lady, go ahead. You wanna go home, go ahead. I rode with Quantrill. An' I don' give a rat's ass 'bout you or your ideas. *Claro?"*

Choate said nothing. He stared ahead at the mountain where Slocum was waiting. He prayed for patience. One more day with Harry Mead was all he could stand. Then he would explode.

He suddenly became aware of the silence. Uusually Sam and George kept up a dull, running conversation filled with reminiscences, dirty jokes, and constant complaints about food, their horses, one another's personal habits, and how they would screw Slocum's woman when they finally caught up with her.

They were absolutely still for a change.

In a soft, deadly voice Mead said, "I said somethin', Choate. I want an answer."

Choate could see Mead's pulse beating quickly in his throat. They were almost at the place where Slocum had killed the diamondback.

Choate turned in his saddle. Mead's two men had their hands resting on their gun butts. Mead's right hand was poised above his. It was obvious that the two men would back Mead if there should be any gunplay.

Choate was good, but not good enough to kill three men in three seconds, which he would have to do if he pulled on Mead. Strategy called for a strategic retreat.

"I beg pardon, Mr. Mead," he said courteously. "My mind was wandering. Do you mind repeating your question?"

Mead let out a long sigh. He spread out all his fingers and then closed them. Then he placed his open palm on his thigh and stared straight ahead, not looking at Choate.

"I said, *'Claro?'*"

What the hell, Choate thought, he could hold out for twenty-four hours. He began thinking of the time when he would

get together a bunch of three or four hardcase Northerners—
not a goddamn man from below the Mason–Dixon line—
and *then* he'd go looking for Harry Mead. The odds would
be better.

"Oh, you bet. *Claro,*" Choate said with a smile.

Mead grunted. His attention was riveted on the dead
diamondback. He held up his hand. They halted.

After they had scanned the area for a few minutes Mead
asked, "What d'you make of it, Choate?"

Choate dismounted. Bending over, he prowled back and
forth across the area much as Joe Charley had done. He
bent down and smelled the urine and the blood. Then he
mounted.

"Here's how I figure it," he said. "Slocum stopped to
piss. That big son of a bitch struck his leg. Then—"

"How 'bout his prick?" Sam demanded. "Knew a man
once got bit there. Got big as a watermelon. Turned black
an' dropped off. For a fact."

Mead looked at him and Sam subsided.

"Go on," Mead said.

"He sat down, cut open the bite marks. He cut too deep.
Lost plenty of blood. Got on his horse and headed for the
mountain just ahead, looking for shade and water."

"So he ain't feelin' too good?" Mead asked with a pleased
smile.

"Not with that big a jolt in him."

"Well, ain't that a pity," Mead said.

So Slocum was not in any position to put up any effective
defense, Mead thought. And the woman couldn't shoot worth
a shit.

"Where the hell's Joe Charley?" Mead demanded.

"Scoutin'," Sam promptly replied.

Mead paid no attention. He looked at Choate. The man

had mannerisms which angered him, but he was intelligent, and his ideas were worth listening to.

"Choate?"

"Yes."

"What d'you think Joe Charley's up to?"

"I bet he thinks it's a trap."

"A *trap!*" Mead snorted.

"Yes. He's probably out there somewhere sniffing around like a suspicious coyote."

"A *trap!*" Mead repeated scornfully. "Slocum looks for a big diamondback, finds one, blows its head to doll rags, cuts hisself real deep, all to make us think he's been bit bad? Jesus Christ almighty in the mornin'! He's smart, but sometimes—aw, shit, I bet he's run to ground up there with that gal lickin' his leg to make it feel better. I say now's the time to move in. The faster the better!"

"You don't want to wait for Joe Charley?"

"To hell with Joe Charley. That man ain't human."

"Ah," said Joe Charley. He smiled. There were no horse tracks going in, but he smelled fresh horse shit. Slocum had gone in with the horses. He had backtracked to the main trail, then brushed out the new tracks.

"Very smart," Joe Charley said aloud in admiration. He would have done the same thing himself. But a man so badly bitten as Slocum couldn't have done the brushing out. The woman must have carried it out with his instructions.

He pulled the carbine from the saddle scabbard. He jacked a cartridge into the chamber. He turned.

Pilar noticed the three horses suddenly becoming restless. They had pivoted their ears toward the entrance. Their nostrils flared as they smelled the strange horse outside. She sat up. She had let the Apache take the pistol rather than shoot him. She had just about reached the end of her courage. And now this!

To stay would put her at the mercy of whoever was out there. She quietly saddled her horse. Rather than sit there and allow herself to be shot or raped she preferred to ride out as hard as she could. The man's aim might be spoiled, and maybe the impact of her heavy horse might even topple the strange horse and rider.

Slocum watched Joe Charley lever the cartridge into the firing chamber. Dust devils were dancing in the desert in back of the strange man. Slocum gritted his teeth in annoyance and allowed for wind drift. These windage shots with erratic gusts were very difficult.

Joe Charley suddenly heard the drumming of a horse's hooves coming towards him. He raised the carbine to shoulder level. The wind suddenly stopped. Slocum squeezed the trigger. Joe Charley flung up both hands. The carbine went spinning end over end. Joe Charley clutched his throat and swayed briefly in the saddle. For a fraction of a second Slocum thought the wind had pushed his bullet too far to the right. Then he saw the tuft of feathers resting flush against the back of Joe Charley's neck, saw the dripping red arrowhead. He saw the blood dripping down the front of Joe Charley's shirt as it trickled from his smashed shoulder blade. A second later Pilar's horse slammed against the scout's horse. Joe Charley slid out of the saddle and lay on the ground. His left foot was caught in the stirrup. His horse moved in a tight circle, dragging him until he died a minute later, choking on his own blood.

Mead's hearing was excellent. He heard the thin crack of Slocum's carbine. A Springfield would have made a dull boom. He knew that Slocum had a carbine. Joe Charley had one as well. The question was, who had fired?

He looked at Choate. Choate knew what was on Mead's mind. "My money's on Joe Charley," he said.

They were both thinking the same thing: a man with a massive injection of snake venom in his body would be writhing in agony by now.

"He a good shot?" Mead asked.

"The best," Choate said.

"So it's the end of Slocum. Shit! I wanted to work on him a li'l bit myself first."

"Me too."

They had unconsciously slowed their pace, as if all need for speed had ended with that shot.

"It's been a long grind, Choate."

"Yes."

Mead yawned and stretched. He had not realized until that moment how tired he was. He had been living hard and pushing himself for a long time. He stretched luxuriously.

"Harry," Sam Hart said.

"Yeah, Sam?"

"Wanna bet he's screwin' 'er right this minute?"

Mead clutched his fists in a spasm of anger. He had forgotten that part.

"An' you was gonna be first, you said," Sam continued.

"I know what I said!"

The thought of Joe Charley fulfilling two of Mead's strongest ambitions, killing Slocum and then raping that woman, was almost more than Mead could bear. And the son of a bitch was only an employee.

The more Mead thought about it the angrier he became.

"Choate!" he barked.

"Yeah?"

"Where'd that shot come from?"

Choate pointed.

Mead dug his spurs deep into his horse. The exhausted mount whinnied in agony, then began to drum wildly across the chaparral.

Choate stared.

Sam said, "Harry has allus got to be first. Then we gets our turn. Then he kills 'em. But he's gotta be first."

Choate said, "What's he going to do now? Pull Joe Charley off her? Joe Charley won't go peaceable."

"I know that. But Harry's got a way o' scarin' people. His eyes bulge out an' he sprays spit all over your face. People who don' want no bath, they back off. An' he's a damn good shot. People know that. Ain't many who'll push Harry if they know him, an' Joe Charley knows that. You listenin'? He musta reached Joe Charley by now. You hear any shootin'? No. So they must be tryin' to come to a nice frien'ly agreement. Like who gets the tits an' who gets the cunt."

He snickered. Sam was much smarter than he looked or behaved. The three men rode after Mead.

Slocum lay flat on the cliff top in an agony of impotence. Mead was avoiding the trap, Pilar was far below, with an Apache warrior whose face was painted for war.

Chato unbuckled Joe Charley's gunbelt and rolled the body over. A fine Colt! The gunbelt was full of cartridges! He was jubilant. He buckled the belt on, and picked up the Winchester from where the dying man had flung it. He rummaged in Joe Charley's saddlebags, and among the odds and ends of a dirty shirt, a razor and some soap, and a little bag filled with needles and thread, he found five marvelous things: three boxes of .30-.30 ammunition and two boxes of Colt ammunition.

Pilar watched Chato in a daze. The Apache pushed the dead Joe Charley around as if he were a side of beef in a butcher shop. Chato looked up at her suddenly with a happy grin. Now he could practice and become a good marksman, at no cost to him except one arrow.

Then he caught the sound of Mead's horse. Chato gave Pilar a quick, questioning look. She rose in her stirrups. Over the saguaro she saw Harry Mead coming at a fast trot. She sank back with a terrified expression.

"Su hombre? Your man?" Chato asked.

She shook her head.

"Hombre malo?"

She nodded. Chato acted decisively. He held up his arms and she slid out of the saddle. Slocum watched all this. He did not know what was happening, but from the way she went without flinching into the Apache's arms, it seemed clear that she trusted him. Perhaps because they were both Apaches? He felt a wave of relief.

Chato picked up the carbine and the saddlebags. He slapped her horse on the rump with the carbine stock. It jumped, then moved at a fast trot to join the others. Then Chato slapped Joe Charley's horse. It had been nuzzling at Joe Charley's boots, and it was nervous at the smell of his blood. It followed the other horse.

Slocum liked all this. No one would deliberately set himself afoot. Mead and Choate would go after the horses while Pilar and the Apache would find a good place for an ambush.

Slocum liked that Apache.

He saw Pilar take the man's arm. Her leg was still weak. She hobbled quickly in and out of the saguaro, ocotillo, and cholla until they reached the shallow gully where they could not be seen from the trail.

Then they went flat. Chato dropped the saddlebags and picked up the carbine. He hefted it with both hands. He lifted it to his shoulder and aimed it. With a sinking feeling Slocum realized that the Apache had probably never fired one before.

And to fire at an expert shot like Mead was to ask to die. Slocum hoped that the Apache would not move.

But, just in case, Slocum levered another cartridge into his carbine. He prepared to fire at Mead the instant the Apache would fire, even though that would bring the others into play and ruin his ambush. He felt he had no alternative.

Mead rode around the curve of the mountain.

A body lay sprawled in the trail.

"Joe Charley!" Mead yelled angrily. "Where the hell are you?"

A hot gust of wind sent a dust devil spinning across the cactus flat.

Mead stood in the stirrups for a better look for that half-breed bastard. He cupped both palms to his mouth and yelled again for Joe Charley. The mountain wall echoed Joe Charley's name.

Mead dropped back into the saddle. "Aw, shit," he said disgusted. He savagely resented Joe Charley's killing Slocum. There were several sets of horse tracks coming and going around the body. Mead was puzzled and a little worried when he saw them. Something had happened here that was confusing. Maybe Joe Charley could put it together. Once more he yelled for Joe Charley.

Then, looking down at the body more closely, he saw two things that startled him.

First, that was Joe Charley down there.

And, secondly, an Apache arrow was sticking out of the man's throat.

Mead was not an easily frightened man. But one thing he did not like was being alone in Apache country. He had once come across a man who had been mutilated by a Chiricahua war party outside Potrero. They had smashed his testicles between two stones and ridden away. When Mead rode by a few hours later the man was in such agony that he begged Mead to kill him. Mead obliged. He still had nightmares about the man.

They had to be close right now. With those horses, they would be watching him.

Slocum saw Mead whirl his horse and ride hard toward the others. Slocum was puzzled, but he let out a long sigh of relief and gently let the hammer down.

"Let's move fast!" Mead said when he rode up to Choate.

"You an' Joe Charley divide up that woman?" Sam asked. "I want a piece."

"Joe Charley's *dead*, you goddamn fool!" Mead bulled past Sam on his horse. "I'm tellin' you, we better move fast!"

"Where's Slocum?" Choate asked. He rode up beside Mead. Mead's head was swiveling nervously, and he rode with his hand on his gun butt. Choate had never seen the man so tense.

"I don't give a shit where Slocum is!" Mead shouted.

"An' the girl?" Sam asked. "She kilt? Didja kill 'er?"

"Forget the goddamn girl! Move, *move!*"

"Mead," Choate asked gently, "what's going on?"

"Apaches, that's what, goddamn it to hell! They killed Joe Charley with an arrer in his throat, an' they's plenty more of 'em around! An' they got fresh horses! An' what've we got? These lumps of shit!"

He dug his spurs as hard as he could into his mount. The

horse quivered and groaned, but maintained the same exhausted gait.

"How do you know?"

The question unleashed a wild, unchecked flow of obscenity. When he subsided he said, his eyes looking nervously into the chaparral and then behind him, "There's a war party out."

"How—" Choate began again.

Mead held up a hand. "How do I *know?* Jesus Christ, Choate, I ain't no tenderfoot, an' I ain't got no time to give you a goddamn lecture. I been around Arizona a long time. When the Cherries go on the warpath they's about fifteen, twenty of 'em. An' we got what they want—guns. They're gonna trail us till our horses give out. Then they wait till we die or get too weak from not havin' no water. Then it's easy. See? Real easy. An' I tell you one thing, friend Choate, I ain't havin' *my* balls crushed between a couple stones."

"What?" Choate said, mystified. He had never heard of this particular way of handling prisoners.

"You heard!"

They were pushing the exhausted horses as hard as they could trot.

"Where we goin'?" Sam asked. He hated and feared Apaches and would follow Mead's lead.

"The mountain."

"What about Slocum—" Choate began.

"Slocum's fer later! If he's in there, we yell, 'Apaches comin'! We gotta fight together!'" Mead said wildly.

"Declare a truce?"

"Yeah, a truce, a truce. We gotta have water an' grass an' a good place to fight from, an' that mountain's got 'em all.

"Suppose he doesn't believe you about the Apaches?"

"Well, friend Choate, then we ride 'im down. The woman ain't gonna shoot; he's still bad off with snakebite; an' when we come chargin' 'im, a couple of us gotta make it."

Choate didn't like it and neither did the others.

Mead said, "Anyone got a better idea?"

They rode in silence for a few seconds. Mead kept glancing over his shoulder. In the distance a dust devil made a brief appearance and then collapsed. To Mead's excited imagination it looked as if a brown-skinned Chiricahua had stood for a better look at the white men and then went flat as soon as he saw Mead turn his head.

"Jesus!" cried Mead. "I just saw one!"

Slocum watched them, He had a good feeling that Pilar was all right.

And here they were, moving into the trap.

Slocum moved at a crouch to the end of the path he had cleared. He set the carbine down beside his boots. He didn't want to be impeded by it when he made his sprint for safety. He ran back at the same crouch and waited.

"I'll go first," Mead said.

Choate liked that. It showed courage. "I'll be right behind you," he said.

Mead grunted in approval. "We'll ride in slow," he said. "One hand on the reins, the other high up in the peace sign." He grinned. "It might work. If it does, we'll all be friendly till the Cherries leave. Then it's four of us, one o' him."

Choate nodded. His strategy exactly.

"That meet your approval, Mr. Choate?"

"Couldn't think of a better partner to share Mr. Slocum between us later, Mr. Mead."

Mead grinned. "Here v are, boys," he said.

He turned right into the narrow stone passageway. His left hand held the reins. His right hand went up high, in his hypocritical copy of the peace sign of the West.

20

Slocum was in no hurry. He wanted to let his pursuers get a good look at the cold water and the lush pasture inside. He did not want anyone killed by the rock fall. He could hardly keep from laughing when he saw them riding in single file with their right arms raised like Ogallala warriors.

The knowledge that the peace sign was intended to lull him into meek compliance suddenly infuriated him. Did they take him for an idiot?

He watched Mead emerge into the box canyon. The men reined up in amazement. It was a lovely sight to any man who had been struggling through a hot and waterless desert. Water trickled down the rock face. Ferns grew profusely at the edge of the pool. A week on that grass would put any horse into top condition, even Mead's collection of skinny and exhausted nags.

The others clustered about Mead as they marvelled.

"This is for you, Father Gregorio," Slocum said quietly, and pushed.

The boxes tumbled into space. Slocum spun and ran as fast as he could.

A dull, heavy *BOOM!* filled the air and the mountain trembled. The entire top of the rock wall framing the stone gateway vanished from sight. Thirty feet of the mountain top on Slocum's side had disappeared. The blast wave had opened the fissures as neatly as an ice pick splits a cake of ice.

The rumbling and clashing of gigantic boulders went on for two minutes as the mountain sought equilibrium. Dust spurted up, higher than the rock walls. For several seconds smaller fragments rained down. Slocum had pressed his face to the rock and had covered the back of his head with his hands. One fairly big stone cracked against his knuckles and bruised them.

Finally silence fell. A thin haze of brown dust hung above the stone gate—which no longer existed. Slocum stood up and walked carefully to the new cliff face.

The box canyon had been neatly and effectively plugged up. A new rock wall, a hundred feet high, now formed the barrier. It was made of tremendous boulders. The wall was almost vertical. Had it been shaped by smaller fragments they would have cascaded down and settled at an angle of repose of about forty or forty-five degrees. Climbing up a slope like that would have been fairly easy.

But now the skills of a mountain climber were needed. There was no other way for a man to get out of that stone trap. Staring down, Slocum saw the four men engaged in a violent debate.

They'd be at each other's throats soon enough, as soon

as they began to realize the extent of their predicament.

Far below Slocum suddenly saw thick brown ropes moving sinuously from the new face toward the box canyon. Diamondbacks can't climb up rock—but they can go down.

When the mountain blew it must have split wide open several diamondback dens which had been inhabited for centuries. Stunned by the massive vibration, and with their home gone, hundreds of diamondbacks were slowly moving down into the box canyon.

Slocum smiled and slung the carbine over his shoulder. He tied his boots together around his neck and began his slow descent to the desert.

Only men without boots could climb out of the trap. And only if they were skilled climbers. But their feet were still in poor condition. They would have to wait until they were healed well enough to try to climb out. Say two weeks.

The horses could not leave the canyon anyway, so they would be eating horse meat. One horse every four days. And if they finally did climb out—which was doubtful, but possible—they'd be in the desert once more. Without horses again. Afoot again.

The delicious irony of it set Slocum laughing aloud.

And it would never have happened if Father Gregorio had not dragged home two boxes of dynamite any experienced man would have avoided like the plague.

The going became easier. Slocum tugged on his boots.

Mead's face was white. He looked up at the wall which sealed them into the canyon.

Choate said, "Mead, I'm going to call you Harry. We're going to be here a while."

He dismounted, lay flat by the pool, and drank. The horses were all drinking. Choate lifted his dripping face and looked at the grass, then at the horses.

"At least *they're* happy," Choate said.

Mead turned and stared at him. "I don' know how the hell we're gonna git outta here," he said slowly. "What the fuck happened?"

"I'll tell you, Harry," Choate said, sitting cross-legged on the grass. "Slocum suckered us into here, then he blew the mountain behind us. Smell the dynamite fumes? You and I, Harry—you and I had better go get a job shoveling shit. Maybe we can do *that* without getting into trouble. Because when we do get out of here, we'll be— Oh, Christ!—A goddamn desert to cross on foot with all those Apaches—What the hell are you doing?"

Mead had pulled his Colt. He had just seen the first wave of diamondbacks heading for the water. He began firing in a panic.

Choate turned. He had never seen so many diamondbacks in his life. They were pouring down by the hundreds now, escaping from their dens, exposed to the pitiless heat of the sun.

"Jesus!" yelled Choate. He began firing too. Sam and George also began shooting.

Slocum heard the wild fusillade and guessed the reason for it. The best part was this: when they would be making their eventual climb out of the canyon, if they made it long enough to try, the diamondbacks would have found and claimed new dens everywhere in the rock wall. And as the men would climb, the landlords of the rock would contest their passage every foot of the way. And the men would have expended all of their ammunition by then.

Oh, I wish I could see that, Slocum thought regretfully.

• • •

Pilar said, "I know what happened. It was the dynamite. Did anyone die?"

Slocum told her exactly what had happened. She let out a long sigh.

"And now we will bring the treasure of the Virgin back to Hermosillo!" she said jubilantly. "You will help me. A mass will be said for you in gratitude. You will stay while I place the robe on the Virgin. Then—"

She bubbled on with her plans.

Slocum looked at her. In her brief time with him she had known such terror and grief that he simply could not add to it by taking the treasure from her.

Shit, he thought. There went the ranch in northern California.

Then he brightened. There would be other ranches, other treasures to look for. The whole damn West was full of treasure.

And all a man had to do was grab the chance when it came.

"*'sta bien,*" he said. "*Vamos a Hermosillo!*"

JAKE LOGAN

___	0-872-16823	**SLOCUM'S CODE**	$1.95
___	0-867-21071	**SLOCUM'S DEBT**	$1.95
___	0-872-16867	**SLOCUM'S FIRE**	$1.95
___	0-872-16856	**SLOCUM'S FLAG**	$1.95
___	0-867-21015	**SLOCUM'S GAMBLE**	$1.95
___	0-867-21090	**SLOCUM'S GOLD**	$1.95
___	0-872-16841	**SLOCUM'S GRAVE**	$1.95
___	0-867-21023	**SLOCUM'S HELL**	$1.95
___	0-872-16764	**SLOCUM'S RAGE**	$1.95
___	0-867-21087	**SLOCUM'S REVENGE**	$1.95
___	0-872-16927	**SLOCUM'S RUN**	$1.95
___	0-872-16936	**SLOCUM'S SLAUGHTER**	$1.95
___	0-867-21163	**SLOCUM'S WOMAN**	$1.95
___	0-872-16864	**WHITE HELL**	$1.95
___	0-425-05998-7	**SLOCUM'S DRIVE**	$2.25
___	0-425-06139-6	**THE JACKSON HOLE TROUBLE**	$2.25
___	0-425-06330-5	**NEBRASKA BURNOUT #56**	$2.25
___	07182-0	**SLOCUM AND THE CATTLE QUEEN #57**	$2.75
___	06381-X	**SLOCUM'S WOMEN #58**	$2.25
___	06532-4	**SLOCUM'S COMMAND #59**	$2.25
___	06413-1	**SLOCUM GETS EVEN #60**	$2.50
___	06744-0	**SLOCUM AND THE LOST DUTCHMAN MINE #61**	$2.50
___	06843-9	**HIGH COUNTRY HOLD UP #62**	$2.50
___	07018-2	**BANDIT GOLD**	$2.75
___	06846-3	**GUNS OF THE SOUTH PASS**	$2.50
___	07046-8	**SLOCUM AND THE HATCHET MEN**	$2.50

Prices may be slightly higher in Canada.

Available at your local bookstore or return this form to:

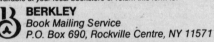

BERKLEY
Book Mailing Service
P.O. Box 690, Rockville Centre, NY 11571

Please send me the titles checked above. I enclose _____. Include 75¢ for postage and handling if one book is ordered; 25¢ per book for two or more not to exceed $1.75. California, Illinois, New York and Tennessee residents please add sales tax.

NAME_____

ADDRESS_____

CITY_____STATE/ZIP_____

(allow six weeks for delivery)   162b